ENCOUNTERS WITH EVIL

101 TRUE & TERRIFYING STORIES

GEMMA JADE

BEYOND THE FRAY

Publishing

ISBN 13: 978-1-954528-45-1

Cover design: Disgruntled Dystopian Publications

Beyond The Fray Publishing, a division of Beyond The Fray, LLC, San
Diego, CA
www.beyondthefraypublishing.com

CONTENTS

I

THE APARTMENT

My first day in my new apartment was fairly normal. My boyfriend had already brought in and set up all of my furniture for me, so all that was left to do by the time I got there was add the finishing touches and make it feel like home. As the hours ticked by and I straightened and cleaned and set things up, I couldn't shake this creepy feeling that kept coming over me. The hairs on the back of my neck standing up, a kind of dizzy feeling and a sick feeling in my gut. It would come and go, all day long. I didn't want to complain at all; my boyfriend had allowed me to stay in one of his empty apartments rent-free when I found myself suddenly without anywhere to stay after the house I was renting was suddenly sold and I was given almost no notice. I had to move pretty much immediately. I finally chalked the feeling up to the fact that, though I've lived in this city almost all of my life, I've never lived alone here, and it was a very loud, busy and high-crime neighborhood. It was good enough for now though, a six-month lease until my boyfriend and I got our own place.

I called James and said goodnight, he was working the overnight shift and a double, so he hadn't been able to come by the apartment that day. I'd see him the next day. After we said goodnight, I decided to just go to sleep. It was a very exciting and exhausting day. No sooner had I lain down to watch TV and doze off did someone start knocking, very loudly, on the front door downstairs. I wasn't even going to answer it, but the knocking got louder and more persistent each time, and finally I relented.

Standing at the door was a young man, in his early twenties. I asked through the door what I could help him with, and he explained he was attending a party upstairs and had gone to the store and was now locked out. Ah! The third floor. That must be what all the loud music and even louder voices were all about. I opened the door and tried to hide my annoyance. It was two in the morning already. I opened the door and moved out of his way to let him up the stairs so I could lock the door behind him. When I went back inside, it took a long time for me to fall asleep due to all of the loud noise and partying going on upstairs. I reminded myself to speak to James the next day. Maybe he could speak to the people upstairs and let them know someone was living below them now. I had to get some sleep; ever since I had gotten up to open the door, I'd had that creepy feeling in my skin and that sick feeling in my gut again. Finally at around three thirty I decided to go upstairs and ask them if they wouldn't mind quieting down. I didn't wanna be "that" neighbor, but I seriously wasn't feeling well. I hoped even if they were annoyed, they'd sober up and be over it by the time I properly introduced myself.

As I walked up the steps to the third floor, I was overcome with nausea. I could barely stand. I was so dizzy. I finally made it to the top of the steps and started banging on the door. I could hear the music and the laughter and the voices. I could even smell cigarette smoke coming from the apartment. Nobody was answering my knocks. I banged louder and louder, each time yelling, "Hello!" but to no avail. After about fifteen minutes of this, I finally was too sick to stand there anymore and gave up. I was extremely angry, convinced I was purposely being ignored. I could've sworn I even heard the music lower at one point and someone shushed everyone else. I couldn't be sure though. James owned this building; I thoroughly intended to have a talk with him about these people in the morning.

The party must've started to wind down about five a.m., and at around six I was finally able to get some sleep. When James showed up the next day at noon and I was still in bed, he was concerned. I got up to make some coffee and realized I felt a lot better from the night before and wasn't the least bit sick anymore.

After I finished my coffee, I asked him about the people upstairs. I wondered what kind of people he rented to, who threw all-night parties, and asked if this was an every night thing. I mean, after all, this all happened on a Monday night. James looked extremely confused and asked me what I was talking about. I told him about the knock on the door and how the party had gotten so loud I had to go upstairs and knock to try to ask them to keep it down. James turned ghostly pale and told me to follow him. He took my hand and led me upstairs to the third floor. He opened the door with no problem. I realized it had no door handle. "Why hadn't I noticed that last night?" I wondered. When we walked in, my blood ran cold. The entire apartment was gutted. There was literally nothing in it except one lopsided picture in a broken frame on one of the walls. James explained he had to renovate this apartment.. A year earlier a bunch of twenty-somethings had decided to throw an all-night house party. This was before self-extinguishing ciga-rettes. Someone had become very intoxicated and went into one of the spare rooms to lie down and sleep it off. The entire room and some of the kitchen had gone up in flames. All twelve people had passed away. As I looked closer at the picture on the wall, I realized, in horror and disbelief, it was the kid who had knocked on the door asking to be let in.

I ended up having to stay in that place until the six months were over, but I didn't stay a day longer. The knock never came again, and I still don't know what to make of it.

2

RESTROOM GHOST

It was another long day at the hospital accompanying my husband to his dialysis appointment. Every week, multiple times a week we had to take the long drive here and wait. I wasn't allowed in the room with him, so until he received his new kidney, my second home had seemingly become this waiting room. I didn't like to leave it either because hospitals always gave me the creeps, just knowing there is a morgue in pretty much every hospital was enough to keep me sitting and reading magazines for however long it took until Gary was finished.

However, sometimes a girl's gotta go to the restroom. I would always try to go before we went into the office, while Gary was still waiting for me outside the door. This time though, I had to go by myself. The bathroom for this particular office was located at the end of a very long and very empty hallway. Very quiet and very creepy. I went into the handicap stall, and as I am sitting there answering the call of nature, I start to hear very loud humming coming from what seems to be the stall next to the one I am in. There are only two stalls in the entire bathroom, mind you, and I thought the other stall was empty because when I came in, I could've sworn the door was wide open. Ok, maybe I was wrong.

After I finished up and flushed the toilet, all the while hearing this woman humming, I walked out of the stall only to see that it was empty, and the door was open and had been the entire time. I walked out of the bathroom but could still hear the humming coming from inside. "Crap! I forgot to wash my hands!" I thought as I reluctantly turned and went back in. The whole time the water is running, I'm still hearing humming. I finished up as fast as I could and walked out, back down the long empty hallway, which was even creepier now because the humming was still coming from the empty women's room. I tried to get back to the doctor's office quickly and without looking back. Right when I was about to open the door to the office, I looked behind me and saw the bathroom door open, and out walked a woman. She was dressed in clothing that looked like it came from the mid-1800s. She looked me dead in the eyes, still humming, and smiled. She then turned and walked through the wall. Needless to say I decided right then and there that I was never stepping foot in that hospital again. Luckily my husband received his new kidney not long after this experience, and there is no need for me to go back there anymore... For now at least.

3

THE PROPOSITION

One night as I lay in my bed during my normal and nightly restless sleeps, I had the most vivid dream. At least I think it was a dream, or more like a nightmare. As I lay there in my bed, I heard a voice calling my name. It was a very deep and sinister-sounding voice, not something I would normally walk toward, but I felt as though something unseen was not only calling me, but pulling me towards it. Much like I didn't have any choice in the matter of going and investigating who or what this was that was calling my name. The exploration led me to my back deck.

My deck in the back isn't high up or anything; you can step right onto it from the ground. As I stepped out onto the deck, I saw what was calling me. It was a very tall man. Well, I don't really know if I can call it that exactly. More of a demon, it looked like a demon. Its face seemed to constantly be in motion and blurred, so somehow I could see his face, but I couldn't make it out. He was standing up against a tree, and all around me I heard whispers calling my name. When I made eye contact, he spoke. "Hello, beautiful night, isn't it? It's about to get even better because we have a deal for you." I had opened my mouth to speak and ask who "we" were, since there was only one entity there; however, nothing would come out, I had no voice. "Kneel in front of me right now, bow before me, and we will grant you every wish your heart desires." He/It then proceeded to list all of my deepest fantasies, things I've never told anyone. He knew the basic things I wanted too, like a big bank account and a new house, but it was like he knew the wants and longings of my very soul. I was almost entranced by him, by it, whatever it was. However, I opened my mouth again and simply said, "No," and turned to walk off, back into my bedroom and into my bed, as I had finally realized I must have been having a nightmare. How else would I be able to explain why I wasn't scared at all to face this thing let alone calmly and reasonably speak to it? As I turned away though, it let out a high-pitched and terrifying shriek. An otherworldly noise that I have never heard before nor since. It terrifies me to think about it now, especially when I remember waking up with dirt and leaves on my socks the next day.

4

THE OUIJA BOARD

I was visiting my older sister in a neighboring state for the weekend, and she decided to have a small gathering of some family we hadn't seen in a while but who lived in the area. Since I've lived in another state for so long, I hadn't seen most of them in a long time. It was myself, my older sister and her husband, our other sister, who is the oldest, and her husband too and a cousin none of us had seen in nearly twenty years.

That night, while everyone else was sleeping and after the party had wound down, my cousin and I decided to stay awake and play around with the Ouija board. While I know now this is never a good idea, we thought it would be a fun way to end the night. While we were asking the board questions, we were giggling and laughing. It was around three in the morning, and we had nothing but a few small candles lit; otherwise it was pitch black. No lights on in the downstairs where we were. Once we had gotten bored and decided we had had enough, we hadn't had our fingers off the planchette for more than two minutes when suddenly it started moving by itself. Slowly at first and then faster and faster. It was moving so fast we couldn't tell what it was trying to say even though we were concentrating as hard as we could.

My cousin got angry and thought I was playing some kind of trick on him; we had both had some drinks at this point. As my cousin looked at me, enraged, and started screaming to cut it out it's not funny, the planchette stopped moving abruptly. We both turned and looked at the board at the same time, and it slowly spelled out "destroy," and after moving around for another second or two, it spelled "home." We decided to just put the thing away. We never said goodbye to it and just wanted to forget about it. It was all very creepy. Once we had put it away in the box, all the candles went out by themselves, and we were stuck in pitch black, trying to find our way to a light switch in my sister's very unfamiliar house. As soon as I turned on the switch for the living room light, the entire ceiling in the kitchen collapsed, and the bathroom upstairs lay on the floor. The tub, the toilet, the floor and even the sink, the whole bathroom had come through the ceiling. Luckily for us no one was in either room.

5

WHITE SHADOW PERSON

She had one of those bathrooms that's in between two bedrooms. I think it's called a Jack and Jill. She closed the door to her son's room but could still see into her room from the bathroom mirror as she undressed. It was the room that was behind her. As she stepped into the shower, she thought she heard a noise but decided to ignore it. The whole fifteen minutes she was in there, she felt as though she was being watched. It was creepy. She stepped out of the shower and wrapped her hair in a towel and dried off her body. She got dressed and went to the sink to brush her teeth.

She wiped the steam from the mirror and saw directly into her bedroom, where a very short, hunched-over figure was pacing back and forth across her floor right in front of her bed. The figure somehow "seemed" female and benevolent. It was still scary nonetheless. The figure was all white, like the shadow people she always saw lurking around her bedroom her entire life; only this one was different. Instead of being all black, it was all white. Like someone took a white crayon, drew an outline of a short hunched figure, and colored it in. It seemed to her, too, that as soon as she thought to herself, "I can't possibly be seeing this," the thing stopped its pacing. It then turned what seemed to be its head and looked back at her. It then evaporated just as quickly as it seemed to have appeared.

It was only later on, after her fear had subsided and she was able to catch her breath that she realized it most likely was her mother. She was elderly and had a hunched back when she died and most likely realized she was scaring her daughter. She never saw the white shadow figure again.

6

SHE WASN'T SLEEPING

I was upset when my mother had moved about an hour away to a sleepy old shore town. I hadn't seen her in over a year and was finally making my first visit to the new house. I had my toddler in tow, who was about to turn three, and my other son, who was raised by my mother, and my stepfather lived there as well. He was sixteen.

Ever since I was a little girl, I had been "sensitive." I saw spirits of the dead and communicated with them. I had had extraterrestrial visitations and even had a family of shadow people who have been following me around since I was seven years old. Immediately upon entering my mother's new house, I got that old familiar feeling again, something in the air felt "off," and my mom noticed right away. "What is it?" she asked. "I don't know, Mom. It just feels weird in here." My mother shrugged it off and took me through a tour of the small house. The whole place gave me the creeps, but I didn't mention it because I knew my stepfather would be upset, as he didn't believe in such things as the supernatural or paranormal.

Upon entering the attic, my mother started to have some kind of panic attack and told me that this was where she knew there was something evil, but she just avoided it by not going up there too often. I shrugged this off, and we went on with the rest of the tour.

The first night, my son and I lay in the huge king-size bed with my mother. My son lay in the middle of me and Mom. The room to our right was my older son's, and the room to the left was where my stepfather was staying while I visited. We watched some cartoons and fell asleep. The next morning I told my mother, as nonchalantly as I could, that there had been a shadow person standing at the foot of the bed and staring at us for most of the night. Watching us sleep. My mother didn't say much about it, and I didn't press the issue for fear of scaring her.

The second night we were there was when something terrifying happened. It was around three in the morning, and I had just gotten up to use the bathroom. I came back into the room, and as soon as I started to fall asleep again, my toddler woke up crying and screaming. He was pointing to the foot of the bed, where his grandmother's feet were, and yelling, "NO!!" It was extremely bizarre, as after this one terrified and extremely loud yell, he fell immediately backwards and was sleeping again. I brushed it off as a simple nightmare, and though scared now, I lay down to go back to sleep.

My mother suddenly started screaming at what seemed to be herself at first, "No! Get away from me!!" and as I watched, my mother threw the blankets off of her and down towards the bottom of the bed, right where my son was just a few seconds ago pointing and screaming. They lingered in the air for a moment as if someone or something was underneath them! I sat straight up, shocked and in horror at what I was witnessing. My mother had jumped out of bed and continued to scream. I tried comforting her, but I was too worried the baby would wake up to actually get up out of bed to try to help. My stepfather was already in the room and had flicked the light on and was in an absolute panic trying to figure out what in the world was going on.

I watched as my mother made two attempts at running towards the door, and both times she was slammed back into her closet door right next to the bed. It was as if some unseen force had been pushing or throwing her backwards in an effort to thwart her attempt at running away. Her eyes were wide open with fear, and she was definitely awake. My mother made a third attempt to run from the room, and this time was successful. She stayed next door with her husband, and I tried to go back to sleep. My mother refused to tell anyone what had happened and just sat in the bed shaking and crying in pure and absolute terror. I tried my best to just go back to sleep, my oldest son turning the light off for me and making sure I was ok. The strangest part is, with all of this yelling and screaming and banging around the room and bed, the baby never once flinched or woke up.

The next morning my mother explained that she had just gone to the bathroom, and when she lay back in bed, she heard footsteps walking next to her side, creaking on the floor. She looked up and saw a huge shadow being coming towards her, and on her legs, sitting there, was some kind of pet on a leash. Perhaps a minion of sorts. I have since visited my mother many times, and while we discuss it often, we never get the feeling it has come back again. What was this mysterious shadow being? Did it really have a minion on a leash? What were its intentions with my mother, and what would have happened had she not jumped up and woken the entire house? I guess we will never know.

7

DANNY

Back in 2006, I was living with my mother and my son, who was about four years old at the time. His name is Damien. Damien would always play in his room alone and talk to who we thought was himself. He would have full-blown conversations and laugh and sometimes even argue with an "imaginary friend," as we put it. All the while we thought he was just entertaining himself as the only child in the house. After about a year of this, though, things started to change. Damien became more withdrawn, and he seemed to be having more and more arguments with this "friend." He said its name was Danny, and it was a little boy just like him.

Eventually though as more time passed, Damien started blaming Danny for things he himself would get into trouble for. If something in his room was broken, like a toy or something, Danny was always the culprit. It got to the point where I was sick and tired of hearing these "tall tales" about this imaginary friend and wanted my now five-year-old to start learning how to take responsibility for his actions. So whenever Damien would blame "Danny," he would get in double trouble. Extra time in the time-out seat or whatever the punishment was. He would cry and insist it wasn't him but the little boy "Danny," who was now, according to him, basically terrorizing him. Danny would break his toys and pinch him. He would pull my son's hair and smack him. All of this obviously was extremely concerning.

One day I decided to put my son to the test. I was tired of hearing him argue in his room with his imaginary friend, and I was tired of my almost unnaturally well-behaved son blaming the bad things he did in the house on an entity I didn't think existed. When another toy was broken, instead of time-out, I sent him back into his room. I heard him crying and arguing again in there and saying, "No! Don't do that. You're gonna get me in trouble again." Well, I creeped and cracked open his bedroom door and peered in. That was when I saw it. My son, sitting on his bedroom floor crying, looking up towards the left side of his room. A large ball, kind of like a dodgeball if you will, came hurling from the closet there on the left-hand side and smashed into a glass framed picture on his wall of his favorite cartoon character at the time. My son couldn't have possibly done this himself, as I saw him just sitting there watching, just as I was, what was happening. I called for him to come out of his bedroom as he swore up and down he hadn't broken the picture or thrown the ball at it. I hugged him and told him I believed him.

As a psychic, I was able to call upon this "Danny" spirit and help cross him over. Things went back to normal for a little while in my mom's tiny apartment above the wicker furniture store. There are plenty more tales to tell of that place though.

8

WHAT IS HAUNTING BERKELEY SQUARE?

In London, England, there is an address that has a very long history of terror and horror but that leaves paranormal enthusiasts and ghost hunters completely unable to explain what, exactly, it is they're dealing with there. 50 Berkeley Square definitely has something otherworldly haunting it, but exactly what is still up for debate more than 160 years after the first actually verified account of something horrific happening inside its walls.

Sometime during the 1840s, a twenty-year-old young man named Robert Warboys was unlucky enough to have taken a dare to spend the night inside the old and long-forgotten mansion. Rumors about the place being haunted and all types of supernatural and paranormal phenomena happening inside had been circulating around it for years.

The dare was for Robert to spend the night in the upstairs bedroom, which was allegedly the most haunted room in the house. He went in with a gun and a candle. He also had with him a makeshift alarm made up of some sort of system of bells, to alert the landlord should anything go wrong and should he need help or rescue. Robert was never seen alive again. It took only an hour. The landlord heard the bells frantically ringing, and then a single gunshot pierced the air. Upon entering the second-floor bedroom, Robert Warboys lay dead with a look of absolute terror stuck in a sort of macabre mask on his face. There was a hole in the wall where the bullet hit, but Warboys wasn't shot. He apparently died of fright. What he was so frightened of that he took a shot at and then keeled over and died, nobody knows to this day.

There was a long series of people who moved in and just as quickly out, allegedly due to paranormal activity, until eventually the house was left to sit vacant. Almost fifty years later the next, even better documented, case was reported. Two sailors named Edward Blunden and Robert Martin for whatever reason didn't have a place to stay on Christmas Eve that year and took up for the night at 50 Berkeley Square. The men fell asleep without issue, but in the middle of the night, Robert would wake to what sounded like Edward trying to fight something off. He later claimed that his friend was being strangled by a brown and formless shape with tendrils coming off it. He ran out of the house as fast as he could and left Edward to fend for himself. Robert claimed one of these "tendrils" was strangling Edward. Robert Martin did go for help, though, and returned as fast as he could with a police officer.

Upon investigation, they found Edward Blunden had been thrown through the window of the second floor and landed on the street below. He had also been crushed. This account is what led many to believe that this entity, mainly because of the "tendrils," is perhaps not a ghost at all but a "semi-aquatic, predatory cryptid" that surfaces from the sewer systems in London.

The mansion still stands today and, in fact, is open to the public for tours. The police have ordered, however, that nobody is allowed to enter the upper floors of the mansion, and everything must be contained to the downstairs or first floor. This goes for the people who work there as well as the public. Probably for the best, as there are reportedly strange noises that seem to be coming from those upstairs rooms. What has been witnessed inside the walls of this very old building? How many lives has it claimed? Is there more than one entity? If only the walls themselves could talk, and it seems as if, until they are able to, we will never really know.

9

THE SOUTH SHIELDS POLTERGEIST

I n South Shields, England, there is a much more recent story of a family who was tormented by an entity that used their three-year-old son's toys as instruments of torture. In December of 2005, a couple we will call "Dave and Mary" lived with their young son "Ben" in South Shields, England. Strange things started happening in their home around this time as well, and it was all very terrifying for the whole family. Furniture moving by itself and doors opening and closing without anyone touching them were just a couple of the odd occurrences happening in this house all of a sudden. Even chairs would be found impossibly stacked, in just as impossible arrangements.

This was a violent entity as well, though, as one evening Dave and Mary were in bed together when Mary was hit in the back of the head with one of Ben's toys. Her husband was right next to her, and no other living person was in the room with them. Out of nowhere, before they could even begin to try to figure out what in the world was going on, they were pelted with toys coming from all directions. They tried in vain to block themselves as best they could by pulling their blanket up over their heads until the phantom attack stopped, but this was to no avail. As soon as they pulled the covers up over their heads to avoid the brunt of these toys, some of them heavy and able to do a lot of damage, an invisible entity seemed to be at the bottom of their bed, pulling the covers off them. The couple fought with all of their might to keep the blanket raised above their heads and protecting their faces, but it was no use. Whatever was in the room with them and launching the assault had supernatural strength on its side. The attack ended only for Dave to find himself with an intense and burning pain going down his back. When they looked, he had thirteen scratches there on his skin.

It seemed toys were somewhat of an obsession for this evil entity because this wasn't the last time by a long shot that it used the toddler's toys to either physically harm or scare the wits out of the family. Once, a rocking horse was found precariously dangling from a ceiling fan. A toy chair was found at the top of the stairs, a stuffed bunny holding an actual boxcutter sitting on it staring down at them with its beady and lifeless little eyes. Ben had a doodle board, and messages would appear out of nowhere that read "go die" and "you're dead."

The entity seemed to become bolder as time went on with the couple receiving emails saying similar things and then eventually SMS messages that said things like "going to die today, going to get you" and "I can get you when you're awake, and I come for you when you're asleep, bitch." Of course the email addresses and phone numbers these messages were being sent from couldn't ever be traced back to anyone.

Toys would turn on by themselves and often roll across the floor, making moaning sounds they had no business making, as they certainly weren't programmed to do so. Little Ben wasn't immune to the entity's wrath either. He was once found on the floor in his room, tightly rolled up in one of his blankets, unable to move, with a plastic table resting on top of him. When these instances would take place, he is said to have been in a trance-like state. Unmoving and unblinking completely. Once the bathroom sink is said to have overflowed with blood, which vanished on its own.

Several paranormal investigators and teams were called in, most probably thinking that this was all a bunch of nonsense or one big hoax by a family looking for a book deal or something. Such extreme violence is extremely rare in cases of poltergeists, and they wanted to check it out for themselves. If they were looking to discredit the family, they had another think coming. They watched in horror as the family had knives thrown at them, disembodied voices came from the toys, and broken toys went off and/or moved on their own and much more. Any investigator who entered the home left a believer of the family. Just as suddenly as this activity started, it stopped, and since then there has been no reported paranormal activity, poltergeist or otherwise, from the home.

10

Poinsett Bridge is said to be one of the most haunted locations in the state. There are legends that say the bridge was built on top of an Indian burial ground and also ones that claim that several of the workers who built the bridge were buried underneath it when they died. The Cherokee people did occupy the land before the bridge was built, so there's a good chance some resting places were disturbed, unknowingly, upon construction. Are these the ghosts that come out when the sun sets to haunt this bridge? Or is it the workers coming back around to admire the finished project of the bridge they started but weren't alive to finish? There is also an alleged slave who was murdered near the bridge who is said to haunt and stalk the bridge and surrounding area.

There are so many floating orbs said to be seen in the woods around the bridge and directly on it, it's only logical to some that these could be the ghosts of people long since gone who had nowhere better to go. The orbs have been reported as being equally as strange; besides the fact there are orbs of unknown and possibly ghostly origin, they are said to be either white, green or even red in color. This may not seem so scary, and it isn't if we only focus on the legends of what is haunting this particular bridge. However, what's reported to take place there is a whole different, and much more terrifying, story altogether.

People have reported hearing disembodied screams coming from the top of the bridge and an unknown female whispering in the night breeze just loud enough for those crossing the bridge to hear. There are cold spots while standing near the creek, and white figures said to be moving all around the bridge itself. Ghostly hands will reach out and touch you, and if you are in a car and try to flee, it's said your vehicle will stall or for some other reason no longer function properly, making you stuck there at the mercy of whatever it is that doesn't want you to go.

A paranormal team named the Ghost Paranormal Research Organization, or GHOST PRO, investigated the bridge back in 2008, and in nearly one hundred of the four hundred photos they snapped while there, there was some sort of paranormal phenomenon captured. The aforementioned ghostly orbs and even a mist shaped just like a man. It was all completely unexplained. If you are ever in South Carolina and find yourself anywhere near this bridge, especially at night, I suggest you get the heck out of there and fast. You may end up being one of this haunted bridge's next victims.

II

THE POSSESSION OF JULIA

I n 2008 a psychologist and associate professor of clinical psychiatry at New York Medical College named Dr. Richard E. Gallagher reported what he believed to be a case of a real modern-day demonic possession of a woman he would only name as "Julia." It's almost unheard of for a doctor to attribute anything to actual demonic possession. These types of things are often said to be the cause of either an overt or underlying mental illness or various mental disorders.

Some of the things that brought Dr. Gallagher to the conclusion that his patient was actually possessed by demons were that she would speak in different languages she had no previous knowledge of or even in tongues. Her own voice would turn either high pitched or extremely guttural, and she was also known to cause objects to fly across the room, completely untouched by her hands. "Julia" was also observed levitating off the bed on multiple occasions and would often shout out personal and private information about other people in the room, often those she had never met. These were things none of these people had ever told anyone, and certainly "Julia" should have had no way of knowing them.

"Julia" displays no signs at all of any type of known mental illness or mental disorders. There were other psychiatrists who have studied "Julia" besides Dr. Gallagher who have also been convinced she was possessed and who have called in priests to exorcize her themselves. Whatever is residing in "Julia" seems to be only bothered by these attempts at getting rid of it. It threatens the priests and people around by telling them that they will be sorry for what they are doing. "Julia" is seemingly still possessed to this day, and there seems to be no other explanation for the signs she is displaying. Psychiatrists are puzzled and perhaps completely baffled by her condition and can seem to find no medically diagnosable causes for her behavior. There also seems to be no medical treatment either.

12

LAW ENFORCEMENT ENCOUNTER WITH
DEMON-POSSESSED WOMAN

A police officer wrote of his encounter with a demon-possessed woman on an online forum where others go to share such stories with people who may have had some of the same kind of experiences. I will be referring to him as "the witness" from here on out.

The witness claims one night he was out on his usual patrol when he came across a dazed woman who was just standing in the middle of the road. She seemed to be in some kind of trance. When he pulled alongside her and asked her if she needed any help, she was completely unresponsive and didn't even look in his direction or acknowledge him at all. As he sat there wondering what he should do next—she wasn't necessarily doing anything illegal that would warrant her being detained, and she clearly needed some kind of help—the woman suddenly started spinning around. The witness then began to think he was being set up somehow and that this woman was having some fun with him and trying to rile him up. He decided he was going to move along and let her spin her heart out.

As soon as he geared up to drive away, she fell down and cracked her head against his police car. Despite the woman seeming to have no physical injuries from the fall, he decided to call an ambulance anyway just to be on the safe side. He said it was a bright and sunny day, and he turned away to do some writing, possibly in his log. When the witness looked back up, he noticed the girl was staring straight into the sun in what he thought was an attempt to damage her retinas. She was unblinking, staring up at the sky. Her face was bright red, and tears were streaming down her cheeks. He thought on the fly and decided to use a book to shield her eyes until the paramedics showed up.

Once they arrived, the woman seemed to have forgotten how to walk despite just moments ago spinning no problem until she fell against the car. Still thinking she was some sort of protestor trying to just wind a police officer up, he somewhat hesitantly went to get her a wheelchair. After the woman was sitting in the wheelchair, the witness says she "struck up an I'm a little teapot pose" and held this awkward position, with her arms up, for more than an hour. She didn't move a muscle or flinch otherwise. The witness claims he called a week later to check on the woman, still freaked out by her behavior that day, and was told she was still in the exact same position he had left her in the wheelchair that day.

Was this woman just suffering from some kind of psychotic or mental disorder or breakdown? Though we don't know for sure, those of us familiar with this phenomenon should clearly be able to see why the witness believed she was indeed possessed by some sort of demonic entity that was trying to get her to hurt or possibly even kill herself. Unfortunately, once again, we may never know the real answer to this one either.

13

THE VENGEFUL GHOST OF CARL PRUITT

I t was 1938 and in a small Kentucky town, a man named Carl Pruitt came home to find his wife in bed with another man. In a blind rage he grabbed a chain and started to strangle her. Her lover managed to escape out a window and left her there to fend for herself. Carl killed himself immediately after murdering his wife. Carl's in-laws didn't want Carl and their daughter buried anywhere near each other, and he and his wife were actually buried in separate cemeteries, in separate towns. Visitors to his grave started to notice a discoloration that looked like a chain with links in it appearing around his tombstone.

A young boy who was riding bikes with his friends threw a rock at Carl's headstone, chipping it a little bit, and almost immediately after lost his life in a bizarre accident. Before he even made it home, he fell off of his bike, and the chain somehow ended up wrapping around his neck and strangling him to death. This same young boy's mother, in her grief and anger, decided to go to the cemetery and take an ax to Carl Pruitt's gravestone. She bashed and hit the stone repeatedly with all her might with the ax and went home. She was found outside her home, strangled with the clothesline she seemed to have been hanging clothes on. This was inexplicable, and many say she was another victim of the vicious curse of Carl Pruitt. It's said that, despite the grief-stricken mother having taken an ax to the tombstone, there wasn't a scratch on it or chip in it, despite it being hit with the rock by her son and also despite there having been cement dust all over the ax she had used.

The next incident is the one that really convinced people this was some kind of curse or vengeful spirit. A farmer was riding with his family in a horse-drawn wagon. He decided to prove he didn't believe in curses and wasn't afraid of ghosts and fired a few shots at Carl's headstone just to prove his point to his family. The sound of the gun scared the horses, and they started to take off. The farmer's family managed to jump out in time, but the farmer wasn't so lucky and was thrown out of the wagon. As he fell, the reins from the horses wrapped around his neck and strangled him to death. For most people who were aware of all of these deaths and the legend behind them, all of these deaths were much more than a coincidence.

A couple of policemen were tired of hearing about the curse of Carl Pruitt and set out to prove once and for all it was all merely a bunch of freak accidents attached to a silly urban legend. They decided to take some pictures near the gravesite of Carl Pruitt. They accomplished their task, but on the way home from the cemetery, a bright light is said to have been following them. It was so fast it was right on their bumper for the entirety of the ride. The driver of the vehicle was distracted by the light and crashed into some sort of fence post. One of the officers was thrown from the vehicle and lived to tell the tale. The other was nearly decapitated by a chain that linked together the two fence posts.

For a very long time no one dared enter the cemetery alone, let alone ventured anywhere near Carl Pruitt's gravesite. The fear they may be next in line to receive some sort of bizarre death by some sort of strangulation was enough to keep them away. By the 1940s, however, one man decided he was going to take care of Carl's gravestone once and for all by taking a hammer to it. He was found deceased at the gates of the cemetery. He had been strangled by the chain that locked the gates at night. Not long after this final death or catastrophe, depending on how you look at it, the graveyard was completely stripped, and Carl Pruitt's tombstone was removed once and for all.

Was this all a series of extremely bizarre and coincidental deaths by misadventure, or was it something much more sinister? Much more supernatural, like Carl Pruitt still being angry even in death and exacting the same revenge he took on his wife on any person who dared try to mock or make a fool of him as he felt she did? That's up for you to decide.

14

THE HAMMERSMITH GHOST

The Hammersmith Ghost is one of the best documented cases of a ghost causing the death of a human being in history. In the early nineteenth century in London, England, the town of Hammersmith was abuzz with reports of an entity haunting one of its local graveyards. There were reports of a figure in white, complete with a glass eye and horns, suddenly emerging out of the shadows. This apparition would moan, howl and writhe at anything passing by that was close enough to lay eyes on it.

A pregnant woman claimed this specter attacked her, and a wagon driver abandoned his ride, horse, passengers and all, claiming to have been terrified upon spotting this ghostly and evil-looking entity. There were more rumors as to whom this spirit belonged to. Rumor had it in the town that it was the ghost of a man who had recently taken his own life and was then buried in the consecrated ground of the local churchyard.

These reports and rumors were taken very seriously. Armed patrols were actually sent out to arrest the ghost! One of these patrolmen encountered the ghost itself and demanded to know its identity in life. Receiving no response and being scared he would be the next victim, he shot at it. Unfortunately he hadn't shot the ghost at all but a man who wore all white as a result of his trade. A plasterer named Thomas Millwood was the victim who lay there, dead from the patrolman's shot. The patrolman, Army officer Francis Smith, was put on trial for willful murder and eventually sentenced to death. Smith later received a royal pardon, and his death sentence was commuted to hard labor instead. (This murder trial was one of the strangest in the history of murder trials, by the way.)

Was there really a horned, one-eyed, evil ghost haunting the grounds of the cemetery in Hammersmith? It's never been proven one way or another. The story doesn't end here though, as Thomas Millwood's deceased body was brought to the Black Lion Public House and is said to haunt the premises to this very day. He is known to whisper in people's ears and bang on the walls. He also walks heavily enough for patrons and employees to hear his footsteps in the bar area of the pub. Perhaps the graveyard apparition isn't the only ghost in Hammersmith, as Thomas Millwood could also be given the same title.

15

PEGGY

The legend of the doll named Peggy varies a bit depending on whom you speak to. One thing is for certain though, whether you believe she is haunted or possessed or not, she is definitely very creepy to look at. On the surface Peggy looks like your normal doll any little girl would love to have back in the old days. It's said though that Peggy is possessed by an English woman who died of some sort of respiratory illness. A paranormal investigator named Jayne Harris claims that upwards of eighty people have reported things like chest pains, extreme anxiety, becoming nauseous, headaches and even visions of mental institutions after merely looking at photos of this doll. One woman even alleges that looking at a picture of Peggy gave her an actual heart attack! This short list is not even all of what it's said Peggy can do to you if you merely glance at her photo.

Jayne Harris said she came across Peggy for the first time when a woman called her and begged that Peggy be taken away. Knowing Jayne was a paranormal investigator, the woman thought she could not only take Peggy but help her with the aftermath of owning the doll. This woman claimed she had nothing but bad luck and no peace after having purchased the doll. She bought Peggy at a car boot sale (which as an American I had to look up, and from the best I could tell, it's just where people sell things out of the trunks of their cars. Like a yard sale but out of a trunk). Many unusual things were happening in her house, which she attributed to having brought this doll into her life. The woman was at the end of her rope when she had called every priest she could find to come and try to exorcize the doll, but none had any luck. She had finally had enough when she became very sick and started having violent hallucinations. Jayne agreed to take the doll off the woman's hands and took her to her own home. Only a few days into working with Peggy though, Jayne also started experiencing strange things and illnesses suddenly. Jayne stated that after a few weeks of being so lethargic and fatigued she couldn't even get out of bed, she also attributed all of this to Peggy the doll and being in her presence constantly.

A friend of Jayne's and a fellow paranormal investigator named Hazel took the doll from Jayne's home, and her health immediately started to improve. Jayne decided to post photos and videos of Peggy on Facebook, and this is where the story took off. The very next day she had more than eighty messages from people claiming that looking at the footage and photos of Peggy had caused them all sorts of illnesses and issues. A medium called Jayne after seeing the posts and claimed Peggy, among other things, "had been persecuted in life." Experts from Jayne's social media group named "Haunted Dolls" made claims that Peggy was "born in the mid-forties" and "had ties to the holocaust."

Peggy allegedly listened when Jayne asked her to stop tormenting people and has even been said to visit people in their dreams with helpful warnings. One example of this is a woman who claimed that Peggy had visited her in her dreams to warn her about one of her cats, and the very next day the cat died.

As always, there is so much more to this story. When Peggy was brought onto *The Haunted Museum* show, she had something over her head to cover her face so that she didn't have any effect on the people viewing the show. It's apparently that serious, the reach and evil of this possessed and possibly demonic doll. What exactly are we dealing with here? Is Peggy the doll really possessed by a woman? Or is it something much more sinister posing as a woman to gain more sympathy and trust while it spreads its evil across the world?

16

DEMON IN THE HOLE

In the mid-1940s at the infamous and now shut down Alcatraz prison, a man was sent to what was known as "the hole." Officially it was "cell 14-D." Inmates were thrown into the hole and left there in complete darkness and silence without so much as a toilet for long periods of time as the last-resort punishment. The hole was called such as that was all the prisoners had to go to the bathroom. They weren't even allowed to wear their prison clothes while in the hole, and they almost never knew for how long they would be in there. It was something akin to a torturous deprivation chamber and must have been unimaginable to have to go through.

The prisoner we are speaking of in this story was thrown into the hole for a simple misdemeanor. The minute the doors slammed shut and the darkness set in, he began to scream that he wasn't alone and that something was in there with him, and its eyes were glowing. The guards didn't take this seriously and did nothing to try to even see if he was telling the truth. After all, how many inmates who were thrown in this modern-day dungeon had screamed and begged to be let out once the realization of where they actually were kicked in?

The inmate screamed all night long. Sometimes it was howls of pain and other times cries for help. He was insistent in his claims that he was not alone in the hole and a creature with glowing eyes was in there with him. By the next morning though, he was silent, and when the guards finally opened up the doors to check on him, they found him dead. Not only was the inmate no longer alive, but he had hand marks all around his throat as though he had been strangled or choked to death.

17

THE GRIN

When I was a little girl, I was always afraid to get up in the middle of the night for anything. I literally dreaded having to get up and go to the bathroom or get a drink. I had my own room, which was great during daylight hours. I remember this one apartment we lived in, every time I would get out of bed in the middle of the night, I would get this overwhelming fear of absolute panic and dread. For no rational reason, I would be absolutely terrified every time my feet hit the floor when I got out of my bed. There was nothing I could do though, as when nature calls, you have to answer.

I'll never forget the first night I finally saw what I've always believed was the cause of this dreadful and nauseating feeling that constantly overtook me. I was walking back from the bathroom. Well, running is more like it, and when I went back into my bedroom, I saw something move near my closet out of the corner of my eye. This wasn't unusual for me, as I was always seeing apparitions and shadow entities. What struck me was how I somehow instinctively knew that this thing, whatever it was, was the reason I was so scared all the time, and I became convinced it was living in my closet. I was about nine years old at this time and a little old for "monster in the closet" type fears. This was real though. I jumped back into my bed, covered my entire body, including my face, up with my blanket, and curled into a ball to comfort myself. After a few minutes of being too scared to breathe, I started to relax and fall back to sleep. It's amazing what the mind can convince itself of when it's scared or there is something we are taught is impossible happening. I must've told myself I was seeing things and drifted off. It was around 2:30 in the morning.

About an hour and a half later I was startled awake. I always knew what time it was because I had one of those old-school rectangle alarm clocks with the bright red numbers on it directly across from my bed on a little end table. I jumped up and immediately heard rustling coming from in my closet. I instinctively knew that whatever I was hearing was being caused by the shadow I had seen earlier, and I was back to being absolutely stone still and stricken with fear. I sat there, stone still, not breathing and unblinking, to see if I would hear it again. It didn't take long before I heard not only the rustling but also what sounded like a low giggle. Normally, being a psychic child, I would just confront these things and make them go away. I would always somehow just know how to do that. This was different somehow though. I took a deep breath and decided to go and investigate. I kind of had to because this felt so different from the usual visitations from Spirit I had always had that a tiny part of me was very curious.

I stepped off my bed and turned toward the closet. I had every intention of throwing on the light and then investigating further, all the while hoping somehow a rat or mouse got in. I'm not sure how I was rationalizing one of these animals giggling, but, like I said earlier, it's incredible the things we will ratio-nalize to keep from going into a panic. Just as I was about to take a step towards the light switch, my eyes wandered over to the closet area. That was when I saw it. I never knew how to define it back then, and even today, with all of the knowledge I've gained since that day so long ago, I'm still not sure what exactly it was. I have a couple of ideas.

The first thing I saw was the eyes. A bright and glowing red. The moon was providing just enough light that I could see the figure almost fully. It couldn't have been more than two feet tall. Its jagged and pointed ears and sickening giggle weren't the worst of it though. The fact that it seemed to be beckoning to me to come to it with one long and crooked, almost skeleton-looking finger wasn't what had me screaming at the top of my lungs at this point. It was the grin. The evil and twisted grin on its face as it looked me dead in the eyes. Its tiny teeth were jagged and sharp and a greenish yellow color I can't quite describe properly. The mouth of it though was what was making me wish with all my might that this was just a very vivid nightmare and I would wake up any minute now. The corners of the mouth reached almost up to its temples. It was literally grinning ear to ear.

Before I knew what was happening, my father was in the room, and the light was flicked on. I was shaking so bad I had fallen to my knees, and I was just screaming. He tried to comfort me and tell me I was having a bad dream again, but I knew better. Somehow I managed to sleep that night, most likely with the door open to the kitchen and with the light in there on and brightly shining into my room. This evil dwarf/demon thing visited me sporadically for years, and eventually I learned to just ignore it despite the fear and urge to scream and run every time it appeared in my closet doorway. I realized it wasn't going to come any further into the room, or maybe it couldn't. I really have no idea. It was like it didn't need to actually harm me in any way; it was feeding enough off my fear and terror at the very sight of it. Eventually we moved, and I never saw it again.

I've never forgotten it though and still wake up in a cold sweat sometimes with my eyes planted on my bedroom closet's door in my new home all these years later. I still won't get up for anything in the middle of the night unless I absolutely have to, and I make it a point not to look at the closet once my feet hit the floor.

18

CHRIS CASE

Christopher Case was a thirty-five-year-old elevator music executive living in Washington in 1997 when he met a woman in a bar on a business trip one night while out with his co-workers. Once the night was winding down and Chris decided to leave and go back to his hotel, the woman invited him back to her place. Chris wasn't interested in the woman romantically and politely declined. The woman, whose name is still unknown, asked him three more times to please come back with her to her nearby apartment. Chris was starting to feel uncomfortable at how aggressive the woman was becoming, so he held out his hand one last time to shake hers after declining again and was prepared to just leave after that despite her insistence. As the woman shook his hand though, she pulled him in close and whispered, "I'm a witch, and I am putting a curse on you. You will die within seven days." Taken aback and figuring she was just drunk and sensitive to rejection, Chris pulled his hand away and turned and left.

The next day he went back home to Washington and went on with his life. Two nights after this encounter with the strange woman in the bar, however, things started to get quite scary for him—and fast! On this particular night Chris had decided to turn in for bed earlier than normal, as he was very tired. He worked out at the gym regularly and as an executive worked long hours. He lived alone and had no pets, so when he started hearing whispering and seeing shadows seemingly running through his house out of the corner of his eye, he thought he was being burgled. He couldn't decipher what the whispers were saying but got up and turned on the light in the laundry room, which was where the sounds seemed to be coming from. There was nothing and no one there. It seems as though whoever or whatever was whispering had now moved to where he had just come from in his bedroom. Chris went back into his bedroom, but, again, there was nobody there and no sign that anyone ever had been. He chalked this all up, including the shadows he thought he was seeing, to his being overtired and sleep deprived. However, this continued all night long with the whispers all around his house and the strange shadows in his peripheral vision. He finally realized there was no burglar in his home but wasn't really sure what he was dealing with.

The next night was the same exact thing, with Chris being kept up all night chasing unintelligible whispers and shadows he wasn't even sure he was seeing in the first place. By the third night he had had enough and decided that no matter what, he was going to get some sleep. He didn't believe in things such as curses and hexes and wasn't a religious or superstitious man either. He spoke to his best friend Sammy throughout all of this time and was relaying to her all of the strange things happening. She would later say she was concerned merely by the fact that it was levelheaded Chris who was reporting these things happening to him.

As Chris lay down to sleep that third night, the house was

quiet, and he did manage to fall asleep after all. This wouldn't last for long, though, as in the middle of the night he woke up completely paralyzed and with a shadow being he could clearly see standing over his bed. The entity picked him up by the throat and started choking him. After a few seconds it dropped him and disappeared into one of the bedroom walls. When Chris hit his bed, he was still paralyzed and obviously terrified, but whether because of pure adrenaline or something else, he was able to fall back asleep for the night.

He woke up the next day and saw claw marks on his throat, and each of his ten fingers was cut at the tips. He finally put together what was happening to him and the alleged curse the strange woman in the bar had said she had put on him. He went and bought books about curses and hexes and how to stop them. He put up crucifixes and salted the corners of the rooms. He burned candles and did everything the books suggested he do to ward off evil and break curses.

Nobody knows what happened the fifth night after meeting this woman, but we do know that Chris ran out of his apartment in his underwear and rented a hotel room. There were no cell phones back then, and Sammy was very worried that she hadn't heard from Chris in days, so she left him a voicemail asking where he was and if he was ok.

Exactly one week to the day after this alleged curse was put on Chris, Sammy got a voicemail message from him where he stated he was going to die that night. She said at first he had seemed scared, but this time he seemed resigned that death was his fate. When she heard he hadn't shown up for work that day, she sent the police to his home to conduct a welfare check. They found the front door open and some pretty bizarre stuff inside as well. The police saw little bits of crumpled papers lying all over the floor. It was later determined these were words and symbols said to ward off demonic entities. They saw dozens of crucifixes hanging all over the walls and candles completely burnt out all over every single room. Finally they checked the bathroom, and that was where they found Chris's body. He was fully clothed and on his knees with his hands in prayer position, in the waterless bathtub, surrounded by dozens of candles all with the wicks burnt down to nothing. There were crucifixes in the bathroom as well, all over the walls. Eventually it was determined Chris had died from "natural causes," and the case was closed.

Sammy told some of Chris's other friends about the alleged witch and everything he had been dealing with in the week leading up to his death, and they all decided to go to the authorities with the information. Nothing changed though, and it was still said that thirty-five-year-old Christopher Case, who was in top physical condition and in great health, who wasn't religious or superstitious at all, who had no drugs or alcohol in his system at the time of his death, had simply died. The woman from the bar was never contacted by authorities or named publicly.

19

THE HAUNTED ASYLUM

One night a few teenagers who were bored decided to drive to an old abandoned asylum on the outskirts of their small town. Of course they had heard the rumors that it was haunted and decided to go and explore for themselves. They pulled up to the dingy and dusty-looking, long-since abandoned building and immediately got the sense that they were being watched. They chalked it up to the stories they had heard about the place creeping them out and decided to go in and explore. They had driven an hour to get to the place, so they figured they might as well go in and have a look. None of them believed in the paranormal or super-natural and thought the rumors were just that, urban legends about a creepy old building.

The friends entered through the front of the place. The doors and windows weren't boarded up or anything, and the place was surprisingly accessible. It was considered private property though, so they knew they could technically get in trouble for being there. They each grabbed a flashlight and went in. The door immediately slammed shut behind them, and they all jumped. One even let out a small scream. They all laughed at how paranoid they were and continued on.

Everything was fairly calm until they entered the second floor. They found a room that had a giant cage in it, kind of like the cages you would put your pet dog or cat in when training them or when they're the jumping type and you're having company over. One of the friends thought it would be cool to step inside the cage and have their picture taken inside. She went into the cage and closed the door, but then there was an audible click. The cage seemed to have locked on its own. It wasn't the type of lock that required a key, though it was unclear exactly how to unlock it. Panic immediately set in as the other friends tried to pull and pry the lock open to get their friend out. The girl inside was screaming and crying. All at once a foul stench entered the room, riding close on a cold gust of wind that almost knocked them all over. All at once there was the sound of maniacal laughing. Extremely loud and terrifying. One of the friends was pushed over while the other continued to try to get the cage unlocked and the other friend out of it.

Just as suddenly as all of this had started, it all stopped. All at once the night went back to being quiet and still, and the cage popped open, again with an audible click, and the girl swears she was pushed out of the cage and onto the ground. The friends ran for their lives out of the asylum and drove as fast as they could back home. They don't have a clue as to what happened to them that night or why, but their views and beliefs about the paranormal have definitely changed since then.

20

BATHSHEBA THE WITCH

Back in the 1970s the Perron family moved into an old, rustic farmhouse in the state of Rhode Island. Their dream home didn't stay a dream for long though as they started to encounter terrifying phenomena in the home almost immediately upon moving in. The couple and their five children would all witness the ghost of a very tall woman, dressed in gray, roaming around the house. The feeling they got off this entity was pure evil.

They actually got paranormal power couple Ed and Lorraine Warren to conduct an investigation in the house, and what they uncovered was absolutely terrifying and chilled the family to the bone. This woman in gray they were seeing was a witch who had sacrificed her baby to the devil before taking her own life sometime in the nineteenth century. Her name was Bathsheba. It seems Bathsheba wanted dominance and control over the family, as she still thought the old farmhouse was hers. The wife, Carolyn, seemed to be her main target. This makes sense, as she was the "main" woman in the household, and Bathsheba was feeling very territorial. It seems the evil witch also felt in competition with Carolyn for one other thing as well, her husband. The old witch lusted after the man of the house, and according to one of their children, she never allowed Carolyn to take up her rightful place as mistress of the house. After being attacked physically and mentally for years in a constant battle of wills with an evil and possibly demonic force, the family left. Rumor has it Bathsheba's ghost still haunts the location to this very day.

21

SUCCUBUS

In Bakersfield, California, a young man named Ethan has what he believes was a demonic encounter. He was exhausted on this particular day but had too much homework to catch up on to be able to just go right to sleep. He stayed up well into the night working on his assignments before finally getting into bed for what he thought would be a restful night's sleep. He couldn't have been more wrong.

Though he instantly was able to fall asleep, it was a very restless night for him. He kept dreaming of some sort of evil being trying to get into his room. It was determined and coming for him. In this nightmare, the evil being had finally gotten in through his bedroom door, and just as this happened, Ethan jumped up in bed with a horrible and very loud ringing in his ears. He lay back down and then immediately realized he hadn't been dreaming at all. There was a demon in his room with him. It was behind his bed, just hanging on the wall. It was somehow holding him down. The beast had also inserted something into Ethan's ears, and his left ear specifically began to vibrate violently. It shook his whole body. The strange and painful vibrating traveled somehow to his right ear as well as he fought with all of his might to break free of the demon's hold. He cursed at it too, but all the while it continued to hold him down as it laughed at his feeble attempts to break away. He was powerless, and they both knew it.

Suddenly the demon stopped cackling and yelled, "SOON!" and all at once let go of Ethan's limbs. Ethan jumped up as quickly as he could and turned his bedroom light on. Though there was nothing in the room when the light was illuminating everything, Ethan noticed his dogs were at his door barking. They were behaving out of character, jumping and scratching at the door. Howling and trying desperately to get to him. I'm not sure whether he calmed the dogs first or went to the bathroom, but when he looked at himself in the mirror, he was almost taken aback. The whites of his eyes were red. There was no white left at all, they were instead the color of blood. Eventually Ethan realized he had been visited by a succubus demon, and he lives in constant fear of when it will return to finish the job.

22

BLACK-EYED HAG

A twenty-three-year-old woman from a small town in Kentucky, United States, reported falling asleep one night and being woken up suddenly by something she couldn't explain. She went to jump up, as one does usually when they are startled awake, and realized she couldn't move. She also felt the presence of something unknown in the room. Unknown and evil. There was pressure on her right shoulder, which felt like a hand, and it was bearing down on the shoulder almost to where it was painful. She couldn't move her body but could still feel that there was something touching it. Wanting to recoil but not being able to is dreadful in and of itself, but what happened next is truly terrifying. She stayed unable to move and in a complete panic for about a minute when suddenly, all at once, she was able to move again.

She jumped up in her bed and turned around to face where the hand on her shoulder had been coming from and saw what she describes as "an old hag." This entity had long, straggly gray hair and a long nose that kind of looked like an old caricature of the cartoon witches we used to see back in the day. Long and pointed downward, perhaps with a wart or two for good measure. Only this was real! The old hag's skin was grayish-green, and she had black teeth. The scariest thing for the witness though was the thing's eyes—they were completely black. No sclera, no iris, no nothing. Just an inky black that, when the witness looked into them, felt like she was staring into a pit of nothingness that almost overtook her. Luckily she screamed, and the hag disintegrated right in front of her into thin air. The woman leapt up and flicked on her bedroom lights; of course there was nothing in the room with her then. Well, nothing that she could see, anyway.

23
RIG 22

This witness reports when he was an EMT, there was one ambulance everyone who worked with him knew was haunted; it was rig number 22. He said he had heard many of his coworkers telling tales of the scary and bizarre things that would happen when they were driving this rig, especially during the overnight shifts. Being someone who didn't believe in "paranormal stuff," the witness just shrugged these stories off and never gave them much more thought. He honestly thought they were all just trying to scare one another and maybe make the shifts a bit more interesting. This was, until the night he and a partner were given rig 22 to drive for the night. This was when he said his whole life changed forever, and his views on the paranormal took a drastic turn as well.

It was a slow night as he and his partner were parked on the side of a dimly lit and eerily quiet rural road, waiting for a call to come in. It was approximately three in the morning, and they were both starting to doze off. It had been a slow night. The witness was in the driver's seat, and his female partner was on the passenger's side. He was startled awake by the sound of a muffled voice and thought it was his partner saying something to him. Without opening his eyes, he muttered to her that he was trying to sleep and hadn't heard what she had said when all of a sudden he says he distinctly heard a male's voice say, "Oh my God!! Am I dead?" This was followed by about a minute or so of heavy breathing.

At this moment he and his sleeping partner both jumped up and opened their eyes, simultaneously turning their heads to the sound of where the disembodied voice and breathing had come from. It was coming from the back of the ambulance, where they brought the patients into. They stared at the empty back compartment in shock, fear and complete silence themselves, waiting to see if they would hear anything else. Sure enough, they did. After a minute or two they both claim to have heard the sounds of an oxygen bottle regulator hissing, as if someone had disconnected one improperly and it was leaking. The witness thought a transient had somehow gotten into the back of the rig and lain on the stretcher, maybe not realizing the vehicle had occupants in the front asleep. This seemed more likely than anything paranormal having happened, so they both jumped out of the ambulance and ran to the rear doors. They flung them open, expecting to catch an actual human being taking a rest in the back of the rig.

When the doors opened and the lights were flicked on, however, they could both plainly see there was nothing and no one there. They checked each bottle of oxygen individually, and none of them were open or leaking. They hadn't been tampered with in any way. There was no rational explanation for what they had heard, and they both just instinctively knew they had just heard the last sounds of a former patient who had most likely died in the back of the rig.

24

THE ATTIC

Our next witness says she moved into a small apartment in Melbourne, Australia, by herself. She was living on her own for the first time and was excited for this new chapter of her life to begin. The apartment was in an old building built in the 1930s and was a part of an apartment block.

After a few months of living there and experiencing nothing out of the ordinary, she says she came home to find something strange in the bathroom. There was a wooden board covering a hole in the ceiling, and it had fallen down, leaving a huge gaping hole leading up to where there was a very small attic crawl space. The board wasn't only lying on the ground but had been broken into two pieces somehow, and the attic above it was completely exposed. The strange part was that the board was about an inch and a half thick and wouldn't have broken just from falling the short distance from the ceiling to the floor in this bathroom. The witness rationalized this and thought that maybe the landlord had forgotten to tell her someone was coming to work up there. She was scared to death thinking some stranger was in her apartment. It didn't matter if it was a worker or not, it felt like a huge violation of privacy, and very soon the fear turned to anger.

She decided to email pictures of the broken board and hole in the ceiling to the landlord and ask why she hadn't told her someone would be coming into her residence to do some work while she wasn't there. She received an immediate response from the landlord asking her to call right away. The tenant called, and the landlord explained that she hadn't had anyone go into the apartment for any reason but also said that the previous two tenants had had the exact same thing happen to them. She promised to have the board replaced right away.

About a month after this event occurred, and just as long after the board had been replaced, the witness states she had awoken from sleep suddenly at four in the morning. She had goosebumps all over her body and said she felt like someone was rubbing their hands all over her body. Everything was still and silent given the time of the morning until suddenly she heard the sound of something being dragged across the attic upstairs. She said it sounded like someone was dragging furniture around up there.

She sat up in her bed, frozen in fear for about five minutes until finally she gathered up enough courage to go into the bathroom and see what was going on. She was completely convinced someone was in her apartment, in the attic. She was armed with nothing but a cricket bat as she walked in and flicked the lights on. The first thing she saw was the new board covering the hole in the ceiling was on the floor and broken in two pieces again. She felt sick to her stomach and was unsure of what to do next. All at once the dragging sound had stopped but was immediately replaced with the sound of someone whispering. In fact, after a minute or two of listening, she realized it was children's voices, and one sentence was being whispered over and over again, "It's your turn. It's your turn..."

The witness turned on every light in the apartment to try to feel safe until the sun came up. It was 5 a.m. now, and she needed to unwind and try to rationally think about what she had just experienced. As she sat and watched TV with her normally quiet and friendly puppy, a fuse blew. It was pitch black in the apartment again, and her dog started making sounds as if he were being strangled. She couldn't see him to get to him and check that he was ok. She had never heard this sort of screaming noise coming from him before and knew something was attacking and hurting him. He was in pain but couldn't bark or do anything other than make this strangling noise. She grabbed her car keys and went and sat in her car until the sun came up. She claims she had managed to find her dog beforehand and put him in his cage before running out of the house in fear.

Once the sun came up, she went back inside the apartment and immediately noticed her dog wasn't where she had left him. He should have been locked in the cage with no way of getting out, and with no way of anything else getting in. All of the windows and the doors in the apartment were shut and locked tight. She was once again in a panic, this time looking for her beloved pet. Then she heard a splashing sound coming from the bathroom. She ran in there just in time, as he was headfirst in the toilet and half drowned. He was only a little dog and couldn't have turned himself around with the panic he was in, and he also couldn't have crawled into the toilet on his own by accident. Someone or something had purposely put the dog headfirst into the toilet to hurt it. She grabbed her dog and dried him off, trying to comfort him, as he was shaking so badly and wouldn't stop urinating all over the place. She had to hold him because he couldn't even stand. He was so scared.

At eight in the morning the witness called her landlord and told her everything that had transpired in the last four hours.

The landlord only replied with, "Oh, wow! You heard the whispering too?"

The witness stayed in that apartment for another eighteen months before having enough money to finally move. During that time, she heard the same dragging and whispering noises multiple times, and the board covering the ceiling had fallen to the floor, broken right down the middle, every time the noises would start. Luckily there were no more attacks on her dog though it was never the same after the toilet incident. He slept in her bed and never wanted to be out of the cage otherwise. After she moved, her old landlord called and asked if she would speak to the new tenants. Apparently they had some questions for her about the strange happenings in the attic crawlspace.

25

HE HAD NO EYES

A ten-year-old boy lay in his bed at night, sound asleep and dreaming sweetly of whatever boys dream of at that age. He was startled awake with the sound of his bedroom door opening. He thought it was his mother checking on him, as she often did, before she retired to her room for the night. He didn't open his eyes and went back to sleep.

Almost immediately after he fell asleep again, he awoke again, but this time his bed had sunk down by where his feet were as if someone had sat down on the bottom of the bed. Not knowing how much time had passed since he woke up to the door being opened and figuring, half asleep as he was, that it hadn't been much time and again figuring this was his mother coming perhaps to kiss him goodnight. He opened his eyes this time to say goodnight to her again but instead saw a little boy sitting there, down at the edge of his bed, and holding a little box in his outstretched hand. He was handing this box to the little boy. Though he was startled, for some reason he wasn't fearful, and he reached out his hand to take the box from the little boy at the bottom of his bed. The other boy immediately grabbed the box back as if playing some kind of game with the witness. When the witness reached out again to grab at the box, the boy disappeared into thin air. The imprint on the bed was still there, confirming he had actually seen a little boy at the bottom of his bed that night. What he remembered, though, drove fear right into his heart and chilled him to the bone. The boy had no eyes! Just black pits you could almost see right into.

Five years and no more encounters later, our witness is now fifteen and in his room hanging out with his girlfriend. His girlfriend got tired, and after calling her parents to come and pick her up, she decided to take a little nap. When her parents arrived, the witness said he tried to wake her up by shaking her. She suddenly and all at once opened her eyes and was staring, without blinking, in the corner of the room above the door. She pointed there, to that spot, and then fell right back to sleep again. After shaking her for another minute or two, his girlfriend seemed to fully wake up. As she got up to gather her things to go home, the boy told her what had happened when she woke up for the first time just a few minutes ago. The girlfriend explained she had seen a boy with no eyes just floating there, above the door in his room. For some reason she wasn't scared of her experience either. She said the little boy was in some sort of superhero pose and just staring at her.

Five years later, the boy and girl got married. Although they moved into a new house, their two-year-old daughter also started seeing a little boy with no eyes in her room. The little girl explained to her parents that there was a little boy who would visit her in her room. He was lost and looking for his mommy. He had no eyes.

26

THE HAUNTED DOLL

A woman claims that when she was little, her mother had a Raggedy Ann doll whose eyes she swore followed her all over the room as she moved. At some point the doll disappeared, and nobody ever told her why, nor did she care. She was just happy to be rid of the leers of this creepy-looking doll and her beady little black, glass eyes.

Eventually when she was older, she asked her mother what had happened to the Raggedy Ann doll. Her mother was extremely reluctant to talk about it but eventually relented and told a horrifying story. She said she had given the doll to the woman's cousin because she knew the doll creeped her out as a little girl and didn't want to see her in constant fear of the doll anymore. However, the mother explained, one day her sister (so the woman relaying the story's aunt and her cousin's mother) walked into her cousin's room and found her having a conversation with the doll. Now, this is nothing strange in and of itself, for a little girl to be talking to a doll. This was something different though, as she claims the doll was actually talking back! The aunt claimed she grabbed the doll and took it into the other room, where her husband proceeded to rip it apart limb from limb. The whole while the rest of the family prayed over the doll as it laughed a high-pitched, squealing sound the entire time. He then took the doll out into the woods nearby their house and buried it. They never saw it again and refused to ever even mention it again.

27

DON'T TURN AROUND

Our next witness explains that when he was a kid, he and his family would often visit a cabin in the woods at the first sign of autumn. They would drive to the cabin on the massive acreage of land his family owned and just spend time in nature. This was a time before video games and cell phones, and they did a lot as a family and spent a lot of time outdoors in the surrounding woods. One of the things this young kid, we will call him Joe, liked to do was drive along the old, dirt back roads to go and chop firewood with his uncle Jim. The encounter takes place as he and his uncle were doing just this.

It was starting to rain, and the pair decided they had enough firewood to get them through a few nights, and they loaded up the truck and headed back to the cabin. In order to get to their favorite spot, they had to drive along these very dark and kind of creepy back roads surrounded by dark and dense woods. The drive back on this night was different than usual. There was some kind of feeling in the air, and Joe and his uncle didn't talk much the whole ride so far. They would later find out this was because they were both experiencing a sort of primal fear. A dread that slowly crept up on them, seemingly for no reason at all and that neither of them could shake.

There seemed to be no reason for this at first. All of a sudden Joe heard tapping on the back window of the pickup truck. As soon as he went to turn around, his uncle yelled, "Don't turn your head!" and it startled Joe into facing the front of the truck again. The whole while his uncle was praying in what Joe said was their native tongue, but he didn't go on to explain exactly what language this was. Either way, the tapping got louder and was coming from directly behind Joe's head. Once again, as if by reflex, he went to turn towards the sound and see what was tapping on the window. There should have been nothing in the bed of the truck but firewood, and admittedly, his uncle's reaction was scaring him more than anything else. His uncle once again screamed a warning, "Don't turn your head. Just stare straight ahead," as he continued chanting these native prayers. This went on the entire way back to the cabin.

When they finally stopped the truck, his uncle told him to run inside and lock the door behind him. He warned, "Whatever you do, do NOT look back!" Joe did as he was told and ran as fast as he could and locked the door behind him once he entered the cabin. After about five minutes, Joe's uncle came to the door and knocked to be let in. They told the rest of the family what had happened.

The adults in the room started praying in their native language and told the kids to get ready for bed and go to their rooms. As they walked away to do as they were told, the kids all heard the adults saying that the next morning they would have to recite the sacred prayers so the evil would forget Joe's and Jim's faces.

What was it Joe and his uncle had encountered on that unlit and back country road that night? No one ever told him, but he suspects it was a spirit akin to the skinwalker, only much more evil. Had he turned around, it could have taken his soul or attached to him. They never encountered it again in all the years they continued to go to the cabin. Joe never went with his uncle to chop wood again though either.

28

SPRING BREAK

A bunch of college-aged young men decided to celebrate spring break by camping on an island surrounded by a local lake. It was in South Arkansas, and our witness said everyone assumed everyone else their age is friendly, so when they were approached by a kid in a canoe, they invited him to come and have a beer with them. The guy said his name was Curt, and though he was super friendly and seemed to be having fun, there was a part of him that also seemed sad and possibly depressed. The friends asked Curt what was up and why he was so sad, and he told them it was nothing and not to worry about it. The friends assumed Curt had been camping nearby and was there to celebrate spring break as well.

Eventually Curt said his friends were going to be worried about him and was about ready to leave. As he turned to get back into his canoe, he looked at the witness and winked. "You don't know how lucky you are," he said as he paddled off into the darkness. The friends chalked it up to maybe Curt was a little drunk and possibly dealing with a breakup or something.

They went back to having fun and partying until the wee hours of the morning before finally passing out. Despite being up so late the night before, some of the friends, including the witness, got up early to go fishing at a favorite spot nearby. A police boat pulled up and asked the group if they were a part of the search party, and they said that they weren't. Their curiosity got the better of them though, and they asked what was going on that there was a search party in the area. The officer said he was just letting everyone know that they had found what they were looking for. The body of a young man who had been missing for a few weeks. He had set out in his canoe and never came back. They found his body at the bottom of the very lake the friends were fishing in. Apparently they had met the ghost of this guy named Curt the night before. No wonder he was so sad. The friends were so creeped out by the experience they didn't even finish out the rest of their week on the island and packed up right then to leave. None of them ever went back there either.

29

THE BASEMENT

A twenty-two-year-old kid we will call "Matt" from Southern California moved out of his parents' house and into a rental house with four roommates in early 1995. The house was a three bedroom and one and a half bathrooms and was not in the best neighborhood. All of them being poor college students, it was what they could afford, and they were excited nonetheless. The crime-ridden neighborhood and small area of living space wasn't an issue.

Matt chose to take the basement as his room. This basement wasn't completely finished but did have carpeting put down and was comfortable enough. There was heat and one of those old-time doors where you have to pull up in order to get it open. His positivity looked at this as he had his own entrance and exit. All of these kids worked part time and went to school, so it took them a few weeks to get fully moved into the place. Matt had only been to the house once before he started moving in and had only been in the basement for a minute or two.

Now that he was moving in though, he was starting to notice something about the basement. Every time he pulled up to the house to bring another load of stuff to put in his room, he felt as though someone was watching him. He couldn't place where this feeling was coming from, but it happened every single time. Once he thought he saw a figure staring at him from one of the basement windows. He instinctively knew it wasn't one of his roommates, but his rational mind told him it had to be. He ran inside and directly down the basement stairs. He searched the large basement but found no sign that anyone had been there recently besides himself bringing more things there. He brushed the incident off as his imagination and moved on. He never did shake the sense of dread that came upon him every time he pulled up to this house, including the sense of being watched.

His first night in the house passed by without incident, even though Matt felt very uncomfortable. There was no reason for this feeling because he had all of his things there, and they were set up exactly how he wanted them. He rationalized that this was because he had lived in his parents' house his whole life, and he was just getting used to the fact that this was his home now. None of his roommates seemed to have had any issues in the house either. It was just Matt, and it was only regarding the basement.

About a week after moving in, Matt was lying in his bed, reading a book, when all of a sudden he saw something out of the corner of his eye. When he looked, a huge, dark shadow flew directly over his head. It looked like some kind of gigantic birdlike creature. He jumped out of his bed and went to run up the stairs, but something grabbed his leg and pulled him back down into the room. When he turned around, already absolutely terrified and trying to understand what was happening, he saw that the shadow bird thing had transformed into a humanoid shadow entity. It had glowing red eyes and what looked like horns. Though it was only a shadow, Matt could somehow see, in his mind's eye, that this thing was grinning at him. Yellow and pointed teeth stuck out in a wide smile as the thing stood there staring at Matt, who was now in a complete panic attack and still lying at the bottom of the basement steps.

Matt summoned the courage to jump up again and start running up the stairs, but this thing was much faster, and before Matt could reach the top of the steps and the door to the kitchen, this demonic shadow being was already at the top of the steps. It grinned again and pushed Matt down the stairs. Luckily they were carpeted steps, but it hurt him regardless. Matt now lay at the bottom of the steps again, this time with a bloody nose and fat lip. He sat up on his elbows, shaking uncontrollably and not sure what to do next. Before he could even consider his next move, this demonic shadow entity flew down the steps and was right on top of Matt, still grinning wide and now pinning his arms down. The entity took full form now and was no longer a shadow but an actual demon. It licked Matt's face with a long black tongue. Its breath smelled like rotted meat and something indescribable. Matt would later say it smelled like he would imagine a dead and decomposing body would smell like. Matt screamed as this thing grinned in his face and continued to pin him down. This whole incident from the time the demon was on top of him until he started screaming was only a matter of seconds, but Matt remembers thinking it had been so much longer.

The thing just sat there, on top of Matt and grinning, until one of his roommates flung open the basement door and saw Matt lying on the ground at the bottom of the stairs with a bloody nose and a fat lip. He would later say it was like Matt was in some sort of trance. He ran down the stairs quickly and shook Matt out of it. It was a while before Matt could explain what happened to him, and it freaked the entire house out. However, they weren't financially able to move and had to stay there. Matt never saw the demon or anything else down in the basement again after that day. In the two years he lived there he would occasionally wake up with a sense of dread and just knowing that the demonic entity was lurking somewhere nearby, hiding in the shadows of the room. He would also wake to the smell of that thing's breath. A smell he insists he will never forget for as long as he lives.

30

THE POSSIBLE POSSESSION OF JESSICA

This story took place in a house in Clifton, New Jersey, in the United States. A woman named Jackie and her two children moved into a new house right after Jackie's husband had died of cancer. The house was old but spacious, and both of her teenaged children would be able to have their own rooms, and there was an attic and a basement for additional space. The activity in the house started right away.

Mainly Jackie's fifteen-year-old daughter, Jessica, felt like someone was watching her while she was in her room. Jessica also felt like someone was sitting on the edge of her bed at night and staring at her while she fell asleep. This was a family who believed in the paranormal and didn't necessarily fear it, though there was much they didn't understand. Jessica said she thought it might be her recently deceased father.

There was other activity such as all three of them seeing shadows out of the corner of their eyes, and all three were having nightmares as well. The thing with the nightmares was they were all having the same ones, and they all involved the basement in the house. Each one of them would see shadow beings coming at them or demonic entities coming at them in their dreams. There was also a woman none of them recognized who looked perfectly normal until she would start to peel her face off one layer of skin at a time, all with a sickening grin on her face. The family would discuss what they were dreaming of with each other, but none of them knew what they should be doing, if anything. Jackie was even a little excited to be having paranormal activity in her house. She was a horror movie and paranormal fanatic and thought it was cool.

After a year, Jackie's son went off to college, and it was just her and Jessica in the home. They decided to use a Ouija board to see if they could contact any of the spirits. They sat at midnight with candles lit and tried to summon the spirits they knew were in the house with them. Nothing seemed to happen, and after three or four tries, they gave up and went to sleep. After this, though, the activity got much worse. They would hear horrific and loud groaning coming from the basement in the middle of the night. Neither female was brave enough to go and investigate. Because they believed it was paranormal and possibly demonic, they knew that the police couldn't and most likely wouldn't help them in any way.

They brought in a medium, hoping to find out what was going on in the basement of their home, but as soon as the seance started, the medium suddenly got up and got to the front door as quickly as he could, all the while apologizing and sputtering about giving Jackie a refund. When she called him the next day to find out what was going on, he refused to take her call. His assistant said he was extremely sick and couldn't get out of bed ever since leaving her house.

One night the ladies decided to take some EVP recordings with their phones, and when they were done, they reviewed the tapes. The only EVPs they got that night were of a loud groaning noise, and when Jessica asked the question to her mother, "Should we go into the basement?" the voice of her deceased father very clearly said, "NO!" Upon hearing this, Jackie decided it was time to move.

She put the house up for sale and was very quickly able to get rid of it. On their last day there, Jackie's son, Justin, called her and asked her who was in the house with them. Jackie informed him that she and Jessica hadn't been to the house in hours and were in fact moving one of the last loads of their belongings into their new place. Justin told her that he had just called the house, and a man answered and in a deep voice said, "Hello." When Justin asked, "Who is this?" the voice on the other end said, "Jessica," in a very deep and low tone that sounded more like a growl than anything else. Then whoever or whatever it was hung up. Jackie was shocked, as she knew that she had packed the one landline phone on one of the first trips.

It's unknown what this was that was lurking in Jackie and her kids' basement, but from what I hear, Jessica has since been plagued with the same nightmare of the same entities as she had when she lived in the house and has even encountered a shadow entity with glowing red eyes and wearing a hat on several occasions while in her college dorm. This story still waits for an ending. Perhaps Jessica will be haunted forever. It's even more likely something demonic attached itself to her for unknown reasons, and unless she gets the right help, she could end up in full-blown demonic possession. I'll keep you all posted. We will have to just wait and see.

31

THE BOY IN THE PHOTOGRAPH

There is a psychiatrist who reported having a patient who was diagnosed with schizophrenia at a very young age and who had to be hospitalized on and off for most of his life because of it. By the time this doctor met this young man, he was an inpatient in a hospital, and this doctor was assigned to him to try to help him through the things he was seeing and dealing with in general.

This young man would constantly tell the staff that he was seeing a young boy, about ten years old, in his room and that he couldn't get any sleep because of his incessant talking. The young man claimed this little boy would sit in the chair across from his bed and just talk to him all night long. He wasn't scary, according to the young man, just talking about his own life and the young man's life and things that went on in the hospital. He would even speak to him about some of the other patients and tell him things about the staff he felt he shouldn't be hearing.

After he told one too many nurses about this little boy, they were concerned he might need some extra help from the doctor, so they contacted him to have a meeting with the young man and his family. The young man was taking his medications as prescribed. The staff knew this because they were the ones giving him the medications, and they watched as each patient swallowed the meds and washed them down with water. It was one of those hospitals where the staff even checked inside the patient's open mouth after they swallowed each pill and after every single dose. There was no "cheeking" medicines or saving them for later in this place. It was a part of the staff's job to do these checks every single time without fail. The doctor was concerned because other than the sightings of this young boy allegedly keeping him up at night, the patient had been doing so much better. In fact, according to the nursing staff and the young man's family, he was better than he ever had been since being on the current dosing schedule prescribed by this new doctor.

The doctor scheduled the young patient and his family for the first available time he could find, and they all met in his office in the hospital where the young man was living at the time. The doctor questioned the young man and his family, and they all agreed he was doing so much better and that, aside from this nightly visitor, he wasn't having any other hallucinations and hadn't been for months. No matter what the doctor or anyone else told this patient though, none of them could convince him that this little boy wasn't real and wasn't really speaking to him. Being aware of his condition since he himself was a little boy, younger even than the one who would allegedly visit him at night, the young man normally would eventually take his family's word for it and agree that something like this might well have been all in his head. Not this time though. This time it was different, and he insisted that this little boy was real and would come and visit every single night. He was positive that it wasn't possible it was any sort of hallucination or effect of his psychiatric conditions.

The doctor became frustrated after several meetings of

trying to convince this young man that the boy wasn't real and, exasperated, took out a small digital camera and told the boy that if in fact this little boy was a real visitor, then surely the patient could take a picture of him that night when he came for the visit. The family thought this was a good idea, as did the doctor, and they all agreed that once the young man could see that there was nobody there in the picture, he may start to come around to their way of thinking finally.

So the next day the family, the doctor and the patient met again, and the doctor asked if he had taken the picture the night before. The young man grinned broadly and said that he had. In fact, he had taken several pictures of this little boy as he sat at the foot of his bed and spoke, very animatedly, with his hands. The doctor asked to see the photos, and the young man proudly handed the camera over to the doctor. All of a sudden the doctor's face went as pale as a ghost when he started flipping through the pictures from the night before in this digital camera. There were five pictures, all in a row, of the chair at the bottom of the patient's bed. To his shock and horror, in every single one, there sat a small boy, no older than the age of ten, in the chair at the foot of the patient's bed. His mouth was open in all of them as though he were indeed talking while the pictures were being snapped. The last picture chilled the doctor and the family to the bone though. It was of the little boy sitting very still and staring directly at the camera, a kind of sly smile on his face and his hand up as if he were waving at the camera.

32

THE JEWELRY BOX

Sarah had just turned ten and was finishing up putting all of her presents away that she had gotten from her friends and family at her birthday party that day. Her favorite gift was a gold locket with her initials on it that her grandma had gotten her. She hadn't had time to put her own picture in it yet but wanted to wear it to bed anyway. She loved the picture that came with it too; it was a vintage, black-and-white photo of a woman on what seemed like her wedding day. Sarah liked the picture so much because she thought it was funny as well as beautiful because the bride seemed to have blinked when the photo was snapped. She couldn't be sure how old the picture was or how long ago it was taken, but she knew it was a very long time ago. Something inside her just knew this about it. It wasn't anything digital that could be fixed, but the fact that someone chose to put the picture into a locket and wear it despite the fact it wasn't the "perfect" wedding picture really touched her heart. Even at such a young age Sarah had always been sensitive like that.

She clicked the locket shut and lay down for bed. Her mom tucked her in and, on her way out the door, turned the bedroom light off and closed the door all the way. It didn't take long for Sarah to fall asleep. Once she did though, Sarah began to have the most terrifying nightmares she had ever had. Though she couldn't remember exactly what they were about, she knew that every single one of them had to do with the bride in the photo from her new locket. Sarah decided to change the picture in the locket from the blinking bride to one of her and her grandmother, who had given her the locket in the first place and whom Sarah was very close to. She didn't throw the original picture away though, she just put it in her jewelry box and forgot about it.

The next night though, even after changing the picture, she still had terrifying nightmares about the bride in the original photo. At one point in the night she jumped up, covered in sweat and shaking with fear, unsure as to what had just woken her up. She heard a noise, she knew that much. As she lay back down, she just happened to glance over to her bedroom door, which was now open about three inches or so. This didn't concern her much as, even though her mother always closed her door fully after tucking her in, she also knew that sometimes her mother would sneak back to open the door a few inches and peek in to check on her in the middle of the night or before she went to bed herself for the night.

As she lay there staring at the door, it started creeping open little by little until it stood fully open and she could see into the hallway. She fully expected to see her mom there, though something inside her knew it wasn't her mother at all. Sure enough, she saw a figure appear, the bride from the locket. Sarah closed her eyes as tears started to pour silently down her cheeks. She wet her bed, and she was so terrified. The woman from the picture was right next to the bed now. Although Sarah's eyes were still closed, she somehow instinctively knew this. She dared to open her eyes just a little bit, and the ghost of the blinking bride was standing over her bed and pointing to Sarah's neck. She was horribly disfigured and had a long, purple line around her neck. Sarah went to touch the necklace on her neck. She was going to rip it off and give it to the spirit of the woman, who obviously wanted her locket back. All at once the ghostly woman grabbed Sarah's throat and started to lift her off the bed. Right at this moment, Sarah's sister started screaming from across the room, she was in her own bed and watching all of this happen. By the time their parents came into the bedroom and flicked on the lights, the apparition was gone.

Sarah tried to tell her parents what had happened, and her sister tried as well, but their parents insisted it was just a bad dream and they should go back to sleep. The next morning Sarah's parents noticed marks all over her neck and asked her to explain. Sarah told them everything that had happened the night before. Her sister told them she didn't see anything except the door creeping open little by little, and then suddenly Sarah was being held in the air, seemingly by some unseen force. Sarah's mother was so concerned she called her mother, Sarah's grandmother who had originally given her the locket. The grandmother explained she had gotten the locket from a thrift store, and because it was so beautiful and just happened to have Sarah's initials already on it, she decided to go ahead and buy it for her as a birthday gift. After her mother hung up the phone, she insisted Sarah show her the picture that originally came in the locket, the picture of the woman Sarah called "the blinking bride," as she seemed to be in the middle of blinking while the picture was being taken, Sarah had explained.

When Sarah pulled the picture out of her jewelry box, her mother was horrified. The woman in the picture wasn't blinking, and she wasn't a bride. At least she wasn't getting married on the day this particular photo was being taken. The picture was a death photo, very commonly taken in the 1800s. To remember the death of a family member, other members of the family would dress the deceased up in their best clothes and have their pictures taken. The woman's wedding dress must have been her finest gown, and she wasn't in the middle of blinking, she was deceased, and they had chosen to close her eyes.

33

THE OLD HAG

A young man we will call "Brian" went to his mother's house to stay for a weekend and had a terrifying experience. This is what he reported. His mother had just moved into a new apartment, and he decided to go and stay a weekend with her to help her get settled and unpacked. Everything was normal the first night he spent there, but on the second night Brian had an experience that would change his life.

He was suddenly jolted awake in the middle of the night, and he couldn't move. Brian had never experienced sleep paralysis before, but he had heard of it. He wasn't too concerned at first because he somehow had the presence of mind to understand that this was what he thought was a sleep paralysis episode and that it would soon pass. He lay there in the bed and tried to go back to sleep. He didn't know that this wasn't normal and wasn't sleep paralysis.

Just as he laid his head back down, Brian heard a noise coming from a part of the room he couldn't see from his bed. He was still paralyzed and realized the noise was coming from a corner of the room he couldn't see because he was only able to move his eyeballs. Brian was somehow able to lift his head, and what he saw terrified him, and he still has nightmares to this day about it. While Brian could lift his head, he still couldn't turn it, but he didn't have to. Suddenly, emerging from the dark corner of the bedroom was a woman whom he would later describe as "an old hag." Brian tried to pretend like he didn't see her, and because he thought he was in a sleep paralysis episode, he assumed he was having some sort of half-asleep and half-awake nightmare and put his head back down to try to wake himself up fully. That was when he heard this woman "slithering" on the ground towards the bottom of the bed. Brian kept his eyes closed and started to pray that he would just wake up and be able to move his body again. This didn't work though, and when he started to hear scratching down by the foot of his bed, he knew this wasn't a dream but a waking nightmare.

He opened his eyes again, and this horrific-looking woman was now standing at the foot of the bed. Her straggly hair hung down over her face, and her eyes were sunken all the way back into her head. Brian tried with all of his might to scream but couldn't. In the blink of an eye the woman was on top of him. Suddenly he let out a loud scream, and this time it was audible, and his mother, who was just across the hall, came into the room and turned on the lights. Brian wasn't paralyzed anymore and jumped out of the bed. His mother asked what was going on, and Brian almost started laughing because he thought now that this had in fact just been a nightmare while he was experiencing a sleep paralysis episode. He told his mother he had had a terrifying nightmare but that he was okay now and she could go back to sleep.

Brian had a hard time forgetting the incident and couldn't get the woman's face out of his head. The image was literally haunting him. He thought about her constantly for a long time, but eventually she faded into the back of his mind, and he didn't think about her anymore. About a year later his mother ended up buying a new house, and Brian went and spent a weekend there with her. Before he left, he explained to his sister that he was nervous about spending the weekend at their mom's house because of what he had experienced the last time in her new apartment. He felt foolish because he was a twenty-three-year-old, grown man and couldn't believe how the terror had come back so quickly when he remembered that night again.

As Brian started telling his sister the story of this "old hag" that had attacked him in his mother's spare bedroom, his sister cut him right off and started telling him of her own experience in their mother's old apartment. It turns out she had had the exact same experience almost down to the smallest detail as Brian had had. The siblings just stared at each other in shock and couldn't believe it. This was a family of skeptics though, so after comparing stories, they kind of just left it at that and figured their mother had moved and bought a new house, so it would be fine. Maybe it was sleep paralysis, or maybe it was something about that particular apartment, but they figured it was in the past, so they decided never to discuss it again and never to tell their mother about it... (To be continued.)

34

THE OLD HAG (PART TWO)

Brian went to his mother's new house for the weekend, and everything was fine, again, for the first night he stayed there. The second night though he woke suddenly in the middle of the night again completely unable to move. Once again he thought he was experiencing a sleep paralysis episode. The only other time in his life he had ever experienced this was that night in his mother's old apartment, and he was thinking to himself he didn't know how people experienced this on a regular or even nightly basis. He tried with all of his might to wake himself up fully so he could just go back to sleep.

He moved his eyes and scanned the small bedroom. He noticed he had left the TV on and thought that was odd because he could have sworn he'd turned it off before lying down to go to sleep for the night. Suddenly the TV screen went fuzzy like it used to when it would go off the air. Then it turned to what he recognized as his mother's kitchen. So the television in the guest room where Brian was sleeping was now showing his mother's kitchen, which was directly downstairs from where he was sleeping. Suddenly and in the blink of an eye, the "old hag" was standing in the middle of the kitchen, staring at the floor. Brian was in a complete panic because he still couldn't move anything but his eyes, and he now knew this woman was downstairs in the kitchen. The woman looked up, directly into the camera, and it was like she knew Brian could see her.

All at once the TV blinked out and turned itself off, and Brian heard someone or something coming very slowly and one step at a time up the hallway stairs, which were right outside his door. He was still trying with all of his might to wake himself up, but he was also praying that this woman was not going to come for him again like she had the last time. Then the steps got louder and louder until it sounded like some sort of large animal was barreling or stampeding through the hallway. He heard pictures falling off the walls and glass shattering from the frames until suddenly it all stopped.

Brian knew what he would see when he turned his eyes to the bedroom door. The closed door started to creep open very slowly, and there stood the old hag. She was just staring at him. She then got on her stomach and started slithering her way towards the bed that Brian was lying on. He kept trying to scream but to no avail. Nothing would come out. The woman was suddenly on top of him with her hands around his throat, and that was when he was finally able to move. He jumped up and pushed this woman off him and started screaming. The old hag hissed at him and disappeared into thin air.

Once again Brian's mother ran in and flicked on the lights. She was terrified and asked Brian if it had been him who had been making all of those banging noises and who had basically smashed every single picture frame she had had hanging on the hallway walls. Brian told his mother that it wasn't him and ran downstairs into the kitchen. He was searching all over the place for a camera. Still trying to rationalize how he had seen the kitchen from the bedroom television and fully aware that he hadn't been having a nightmare or a sleep paralysis episode, he was absolutely terrified. His mother asked him what he was doing and explained she didn't have a camera in her kitchen. There were no cameras inside her house.

Brian then sat his mother down, and after calming himself down, he explained to his worried mother what had happened to him not only this time, but the last time he had slept over at her apartment as well. His mother was shocked and horrified and told him, in full detail, how she had had the exact same experiences as Brian and his sister had had and that had actually been the reason she moved from the apartment to the house. No one in the family ever had an encounter with the old hag again and have no idea what they experienced or why. One thing they all agree on, though? It definitely wasn't sleep paralysis or a nightmare. It was real and happening while they were awake.

35

DON'T PULL OVER

A girl named Tammy and her mother were driving home from her cheerleading practice on the lonely and desolate back roads that led to their house in the country. They lived in the middle of nowhere, and the roads leading there could become extremely dark once the sun went down because there were very few streetlights on them. The mother was speeding just a little bit, trying to get them home before it got dark. She hated driving these unlit and pitch-black roads at night. As the sun went down and darkness started to fall, and as Tammy's mom got more and more frustrated she wasn't going to get them home before full dark, she started to drive even faster down these windy and deserted back roads.

Tammy didn't like being on these roads at night either. They were surrounded by nothing but deep and dense woods, and to be honest, they gave her the creeps. She tried to distract herself by watching the trees go by and humming to herself. The car was quiet when all of a sudden Tammy thought she saw a young girl walking down the side of these unlit and desolate roads. She wasn't sure, so she turned her head as her mom sped by and saw the girl out of the back window of the car. Tammy told her mother to stop and explained what she had seen. Her mother didn't believe her, but Tammy insisted, and they both knew that, despite not wanting to be on these creepy back roads any longer than absolutely necessary to get home, they had to turn around. There were no houses and no civilization for miles, and there was no reason a young girl should be out walking around out there. It was also the dead of winter and very cold outside.

Her mother begrudgingly made a U-turn, and they decided to go and see if the girl needed any help. As soon as her mother started driving in the opposite direction, however, a strange and unexplained terror washed over Tammy, and she started begging her mother not to go and find the girl but to just turn back around and go home. Her mother's maternal instincts had already kicked in though, and the thought of leaving a young girl out on these roads at night in the freezing cold just wasn't an option.

Tammy was so terrified she was crying and screaming at her mother not to approach this young girl, and then they saw her. She was still walking, this time on the opposite side of the road and away from them. Tammy was so scared, she crawled down into the little space between the front seat and the front of the car and covered her eyes. Of course her mother thought she was being ridiculous, as the whole time her mother turned around again to stop and ask this young girl if she needed help, Tammy bawled her eyes out and pleaded with her mother to just keep going and leave this girl alone. Neither of them knew where this sudden terror was coming from.

After her mother turned around, she slowed down and leaned her arm over to manually roll down Tammy's window after Tammy had refused to take her hands off her eyes or get back up in her seat. The mother did notice something very strange right off the bat. This young girl didn't even react to a strange car pulling up to her on the side of the road and slowing down beside her. The girl was walking kind of oddly as well, but still the mother rolled the window down and asked if the girl needed any help. Right after she asked the question, she took off like a bat out of hell and started screaming, crying and praying all at once and out loud. Now that the car was moving back in the direction of home and in the opposite direction of this young girl, Tammy felt safe enough to get back in her seat despite her mother's sudden and bizarre behavior. She kept asking her mother what happened, but her mother refused to answer her.

Once they got home, her mother told her to run, and she did, and once they were in the house, her mother went around and locked all of the doors and windows. Finally she told Tammy what had happened when she'd asked the young girl if she needed any help. "She turned and looked at me, and she had no face!! She had no face!!"

36

ANNIE'S ROAD

Growing up in a rural part of Northern New Jersey, there wasn't really much to do. I was always a fan of horror movies and all things that go bump in the night. Being a psychic teenager will do that to you. It was the '90s, and *The Craft* was a very popular movie at the time. Spooky was cool, and one night a few of my friends and I were up for a bit of a scare. We thought we were going to have some innocent fun while debunking a local urban legend all at once.

The legend of Annie's Road differs depending on whom you're asking, but I will tell you the legend I have heard the most. Annie was not very popular in school and was in fact relentlessly bullied. Just like in the movie *Carrie*, she was asked to prom by the most popular guy in school and agreed to go. Little did she know after he picked her up, his friends were in the back seat. They were all drunk, and they all had their way with her. When they were done, they dumped her out on the side of the road, where she was hit by a semi and decapitated. Legend has it she roams Riverview Drive in Totowa, New Jersey, looking for not just her head, but for the ancestors of the men who did this to her that fateful night. This is, of course, the very short version. There are too many legends about what will happen if you travel Annie's Road at midnight and especially if you stop your car.

One night my friends and I decided to drive down it at midnight, and right in the middle of nowhere on this lonely and desolate stretch of road, we stopped the car and turned it off. We just waited there in the silence on the side of the road. We were laughing and giggling at the innocent terror of it all. That's when all at once it seemed as though our car was being shaken or rocked from all sides. We had started to scream, and all four of us looked around in horror, trying to see the culprit who was shaking our car like this. My friend was trying to start the car, but it wouldn't turn over. It seemed like the engine or battery was dead. We heard cackling laughter and then silence. Though it seemed the shaking of the vehicle and horrific laughter lasted an hour, it was really only about a minute.

Just as suddenly as it had started, it all stopped. My friend turned the key, and the car started with no problem. As she sped off into the night, all of us terrified and crying our eyes out, we heard an animalistic scream. It was inhuman, and for me, it was the scariest part of the night. We all stayed at my house that night, but none of us slept very well.

When I walked my friends back out to the car the next day, there were claw marks all over the sides and the trunk. We hadn't thought to look the night before after the incident on Annie's Road, but we knew for sure they weren't there before we took that ride. We eventually decided to stop talking about it, and none of us ever brought it up again after that first day. I still have no idea what we encountered that night.

As an adult, "Annie's Road," which is really Riverview Drive, is where my church is. Every Sunday I have to drive along the road and remember the terror I felt that night. Every time it's fresh and new. I make it a point to never drive that road at night for any reason and am seriously considering finding an alternate route to services on Sunday.

37
DEATH CALLING

Somewhere in the midwestern United States not too long ago, an old woman called 911 and was screaming for help. She was an old widow, and the dispatchers knew her well. This elderly lady would call 911 multiple times a week and scream into the phone for her long-since-deceased husband to help her. Dispatch would see her address and number come up and know it was her, and they even had a whole protocol set for when these calls would come in. After listening to her immediately start screaming, "John, help me!" (John was the name of her deceased husband) the dispatchers would explain to her that she was calling 911 and that her husband had passed away long ago. They would advise her to call her family if she needed help, but the calls persisted anyway. Because the old woman was screaming for help, the dispatchers had no choice but to send a patrol car to the woman's house every single time.

They did this for a while, but eventually, after officers went to her home multiple times a week for months and months, they decided to calmly explain to her that her husband was deceased, and she needed to stop calling an emergency service line asking for him. They also stopped sending patrol cars to her house every time she called. Eventually the old woman died peacefully in her sleep, and the news somehow made it back to the dispatchers. They were a bit sad that the senile old woman would no longer be making their lives more interesting each night with her frantic and seemingly random calls to 911. The officers who were sent to her home so often mourned a bit as well. They were all a bit relieved too though, now the incessant calls would finally stop. Or so they thought.

About a week after the old woman was dead and buried, the 911 dispatcher on duty that night saw her number and address come up on the line when the phone rang. Thinking it was some sort of mistake and knowing she was deceased now, the operator decided to pick up the call anyway and see what happened. She got the shock of her life when in her ear, clear as day, was the old woman yelling her usual pleas to her long-deceased husband, John, "Help me, John!" The operator was experiencing a bit of shock and hung up the phone quickly. The other employees who were working with her that night tried to convince her it was some sort of prank. The operator knew better though. They had been receiving those calls every single week, all week long, for more than a year. They all knew the old woman's voice and tone very well.

For the next month these calls from the old woman continued to come into the dispatch center, and eventually, thinking there was some kind of prank going on, officers were dispatched to the house and went in. The house was completely empty, and nobody was there.

They called the phone company to see if the line still belonged to the old woman because they suspected that transients or teenagers were breaking into the house and making these calls. The idea was extremely far-fetched, but they figured it was much more possible than the alternative, which was that the old woman was somehow making the calls herself from the afterlife. The phone company told the officer who called that the old woman's number had been disconnected almost immediately upon her passing away.

The dispatchers and officers were all stumped, yet the calls continued week after week for several months. Eventually the old woman's house burned down, and still, there were calls coming in from her on an almost nightly basis now, asking for her husband and screaming into the receiver for him to come and help her. Nobody knew what to do, but they had to answer the calls every time they came in because there was a chance someone could actually be in need of emergency assistance. It was scary and confusing for all involved.

Eventually the calls became more and more infrequent until they stopped altogether. It's never been explained, and nobody knows for sure how this could have happened. Those involved who grew fond of the old lady like to think that she found her dear departed husband on the other side and therefore didn't need his help anymore. However, we most likely will never know the truth about this one either.

38

IMAGINARY FRIEND

A young girl named Molly moved across the country with her family, from Oregon to New Jersey, when she was ten years old. Being the new girl in the neighborhood at that age automatically made her an outcast, and of the few kids on her block who were the same age as her, Molly couldn't get any of them to want to be her friend. It was summertime when she moved, and one of the things she most liked doing was going into the woods near her house and exploring. She did this almost every day, and her parents didn't mind because she was always home on time, and also, they lived in a very safe community. This was also the 1980s and so was a different time from now. Kids played outside until the streetlights came on, and that was that. There was very little adult supervision.

Molly was out on one of her adventures in the woods one day when she saw another little girl, about her age, also wandering the woods and seemingly exploring, just as she was. The other little girl held a blue stuffed teddy bear, and Jessica immediately noticed the other girl's dress. It was much different than anything she had ever seen before. The other girl approached her and introduced herself as Lisa. Lisa and Molly became quick friends and would meet in the woods almost every day after this.

Molly eventually brought Lisa home with her and even introduced her to her parents. Lisa would stay for dinner and spend the night all the time. At the age of ten it never occurred to Molly why she was never invited to Lisa's house or why she had never met Lisa's parents. One night Lisa was spending the night, and she and Molly were up very late talking and giggling, as young girls will do. Molly's father yelled for Molly to stop giggling and go to sleep several times. After a while he got frustrated and went into Molly's room to reprimand her. It was two o'clock in the morning, and she was still up whispering and giggling with Lisa. Molly's father then insisted that Lisa had to go home. Molly started crying and was confused because it was so late. This is when her father explained to her that Lisa was not real, and he was sick and tired of playing make-believe and that Molly had to start taking responsibility for her own actions. Actions such as staying up too late and talking and giggling to herself.

Molly was shocked because she knew Lisa was real. She had spent every day that summer with her. Molly's father got angrier by the minute as she continued to insist that Lisa was real. By this time both Molly and Lisa were crying, and Molly's father shouted, "Lisa, you have to leave, and I don't ever want you to come back here again." In his anger and frustration he was simply trying to prove a point to his daughter. After working all day and considering the time, it's fair to assume he was also just exhausted and wanted to get some sleep. Molly was beside herself as Lisa stood up and walked out of her room. Lisa turned around one more time, with tears in her eyes, and blew a kiss to Molly.

Molly's father left the room after giving a final warning to Molly to go to sleep and after reiterating one more time that

Lisa was no longer welcome in their house. Molly's father later reported that as he left Molly's room, he went back into his room and was sitting on the side of his bed, feeling guilty for yelling at his daughter. He stood up and walked into the hallway, which led to her room, and went to apologize to her and tuck her in for sleep one more time. As he opened his bedroom door though, he happened to look to his right, away from Molly's room, which was on the left, and to his shock he saw a little girl in an old-fashioned dress, clutching an old raggedy blue teddy bear. The girl had tears streaming down her face, and she gave him a mean look. She then disappeared through the front door. She had walked right through the door!

He ran to the door, his heart pounding, and opened it to look and see if he had indeed just seen a little girl walk through his front door. Perhaps he thought she had somehow opened it and he was overtired. Whatever the case was, there was nobody out there in the frigid and dark night. He then felt a huge wave of guilt and pleaded for Lisa to come back and said it was okay if she stayed and played with Molly, but neither he nor Molly ever saw the little girl again.

Molly was too young to understand she had been playing with a ghost, but she did have a terrible nightmare that night. She dreamt of Lisa in the woods where they had first met. She was running and seemed to be in fear for her life. There were men chasing her, and eventually they caught up with her. The nightmare was a blur of images, and some seemed to just slip by while others were very clear. The last image Molly remembered seeing was of one of the men picking up a large rock and smashing Lisa in the head with it as she loosened her grasp on her blue teddy bear.

39

BEYOND THE MURDERS

I n Villisca, Iowa, in the early 1900s a gruesome murder took place that was never solved. Due to the weapon chosen by the still unknown perpetrator, the house in which this all happened is known to this day as "The Villisca Axe Murder House." Today the home still stands and is a museum of the macabre. It is known far and wide for being extremely haunted, and by some very sinister spirits. The murderer allegedly appears in shadow, still wielding his ax, and the sounds of disembodied children's laughter and screams can be heard throughout the place.

Before it was turned into a museum, many tenants have come and gone through its doors, never being able to stay for more than a month or two because of all of the terrifying activity that went on almost nonstop from the time someone would move in until the time they would move out. There is an ominous presence in the house, as though the house itself is malevolent and just waiting for the right time to strike. The attic is where most of the evil activity is said to occur. Many ghost hunters and psychics have come and gone through its doors as well over the years. Even in more recent years, it seems as though the house hasn't slowed down a bit and is allegedly responsible for several attacks on human beings who were there for one reason or another.

In 2014 a thirty-seven-year-old man named Robert Steven Laursen Jr. was there on an amateur ghost-hunting mission with a few of his friends. His friends reported later that at around 12:45 a.m., Robert suddenly began to panic and yell unintelligibly into his walkie-talkie, apparently trying to alert his friends, who were all somewhere else exploring in other parts of the house, that he needed some sort of help. His friends eventually found him, and he seemed to have self-inflicted stab wounds to his chest, which he said were the result of someone or something taking over his mind and body and forcing him to do this to himself. It should be noted here that 12:45 a.m. is approximately the same time the original murders took place in the house.

Robert Laursen's condition once he was admitted in the hospital was never publicly released, and trying to find out if he survived has been harder than one would think. Was this the case of a malevolent, supernatural entity who got tired of people poking around its home and took matters into its own otherworldly hands, or simply a case of a publicity stunt? That's for each individual to decide, I suppose. I would point people to the fact that, as I previously mentioned, I can't find much if any information about Robert Laursen after the stabbing at the house, despite specifically searching and having the entire internet at my disposal. If this were a publicity stunt, I think he would have made more of a public show of what happened to him that night and maybe made some money off of it. As far as I know, he didn't. You can pay $428 per night to stay at the house either by yourself or with up to five members of your ghost-hunting team or friends.

40

ROCKING HORSE

S hannon was around ten years old when she experienced what she refers to as "the rocking horse incident," and I'll never forget how scared she was when she recounted the story to me about ten years later on our first night in our new apartment. She was my best friend, and we went to the same college and decided to live off campus together. The wine was flowing, and we were bored of whatever was on television in 2003. (I'm pretty sure streaming didn't exist back then, and if it did, we didn't know anything about it.) We started talking about our favorite horror movies, and the conversation kind of progressed from there into paranormal experiences. She knew I am a lifelong experiencer and loved when I would tell her my stories.

This night, though, she surprised me when she told me she had a story of her own to tell. She explained she'd thought of it because her sister was about to give birth, and her mother had asked her if she would be willing to look in the attic for some of their baby toys for the new arrival. Specifically, her mother had asked for the rocking horse, which she and her sister had had in their room from birth until Shannon was seventeen years old.

She had insisted her parents get rid of it one day, seemingly randomly and out of nowhere, and she hadn't known it had been in the attic the whole time. She had hoped to be rid of it forever, never to see it again.

She said it happened one night when she was lying in her bed and her sister was out at a sleepover. The night was pretty normal, and Shannon eventually went up into her second-floor bedroom to play with her toys for a few minutes before going to sleep. When she went into her room, she noticed immediately that one of her dolls wasn't where she always kept it on her bed and was instead in the corner, on top of an old rocking horse she and her sister never used anymore. It always gave them the creeps, but being little kids, they didn't know how to explain the "off" feelings and instead just stuck it in a corner of the room and never used or played with it. That was what made the fact odd that one of her most favorite dolls was over on this chair, essentially looking like it was riding on the horse. The doll wasn't just placed there, it was in a riding position with hands reaching towards the two knobs near the horse's ears where a child would hold on in order to rock on it. Immediately being scared, Shannon ran over to the horse and snatched her doll off it. She then went to her bed and lay with the doll to go to sleep.

A few minutes later her mother came in to check on her and tuck her in, and all she was left with was a tiny sliver of light coming in from the hallway into her pitch-black room. She kept thinking about the rocking horse and was becoming more and more scared. However she finally did fall asleep, though it was quite a while after she lay down.

In the middle of the night, Shannon woke up to the sound of a creaking noise coming from a corner of her bedroom. The corner where the rocking horse was. Immediately terrified, she clutched her doll and pulled the covers up over her head for fear of what she might see. Though the room was pitch black, she just sensed someone or something was in there with her. Eventually the creaking sound revealed itself to be the familiar rocking of the horse on the hardwood bedroom floor. Then the sound got closer and closer; all the while Shannon lay with her head under the covers and in a fetal position, frozen in place and in fear. She couldn't even call out for her parents; she was too afraid of whatever was making the rocking chair move like that. It sounded like it was gliding across the floor and coming towards her bed. She started to pray in whispers as tears streamed down her face, and the next thing she knew, it was morning. She had somehow fallen asleep.

As she flung the covers off her face and went to race downstairs to tell her mother what had happened, what she had thought she heard the night before, she stopped dead in her tracks the second her feet hit the floor. There was the rocking horse. It was no longer in the corner but in the middle of the room, right at the foot of her bed, and on it sat her favorite doll, the same one she had taken to bed with her that night. She looked to her bed, and sure enough, the doll was missing. Shannon never told anyone about the experience until the night she told me all those years later. She said she never had another encounter neither before nor since. She did say, however, that any other time her sister slept at a friend's house or was otherwise out for the evening, she would pretend to be staying up late watching movies so she could just sleep on the couch without being questioned about it.

Finally when she was seventeen and her sister was twenty-two and moving out to begin her own life, Shannon insisted to her mother to get rid of the rocking horse, claiming she had long since outgrown it. I didn't say much, and we kind of both didn't feel much like doing anything after that, so we went to bed. I lost touch with Shannon soon after when she left school and had to go home to help her sister with the new baby, who was now a little over a year old. It seems her brother-in-law had had some kind of accident coming out of the little girl's room. He was screaming something and slipped while running down the stairs and away from what seemed like something he saw in the room. Nobody will ever know though, as he passed away. I wonder though, I really do...

41

HOSPITAL GOBLINS

My stepfather recently told me a story from when he was hospitalized for about a month in a local hospital here in southern New Jersey. He said that once he left the ICU and was taken off several of his medications, he had a clear head again and was excited because he was closer to being released. While he was in the ICU and on all of the medications, he said he would hallucinate that little green "monsters" with long, fat tails would crawl all over the radiator and down on the floor by the foot of his bed, but because of the medications, he knew he was hallucinating and paid it no mind. Once he was moved into a regular hospital room, he figured these creatures wouldn't follow because he would no longer be hallucinating.

My stepfather is a lifelong nonbeliever in anything supernatural, extraterrestrial or paranormal and actually thinks it is all make-believe and figments of overactive imaginations. However, when night came and he was in his regular room and watching television, he said he must have dozed off. When he woke up, it was the middle of the night, and sure enough, these little creatures, which he referred to as goblins, were there crawling all over his radiator and on the floor at the foot of his bed. He said they were the size of a small kitten, and there were about forty of them altogether. He was shocked and couldn't believe his eyes. He said all he could do was watch them running back and forth, but after a while it was like they noticed him staring at them. They noticed he could see them. Once that happened, he explained, they all congregated at the side of his bed and started jumping, trying to get to him. He finally decided to continue trying to watch the TV and ignored them altogether. Eventually he said they went away, but every night for the rest of his stay, they came back and always tried to jump into the bed.

I have seen before where people have encountered similar creatures in their homes, and they were demonic and would crawl into beds and take bites out of the people they were running around. Luckily this didn't happen to my stepfather, and I never told him what I knew about these little creatures from hell.

42

DEVILS OF DEATH

A friend of mine was staying in the hospital for a few months, recovering from a very bad car accident. I made it a point to call him every night to make sure he was okay and feeling better. I couldn't go and visit him, as with the pandemic going on in our country, the visiting rules went from extremely strict to nonexistent in a very short period of time.

After he was there for a month or so, our nighttime conversations started to change. He started to tell me about men in top hats who would walk back and forth in front of the door to his room every night. It was almost like they were walking in one big circle around the nurses' station, but whenever they would walk past his room, they would peek their heads in and stare at him for a minute. He always pretended he didn't see them but told me he was terrified because although they looked like men in most ways, their faces were another story. He described the faces as "ghoulish and ever changing." I have heard of this kind of thing before, and in my opinion these beings are devils of death. I gave them this name because I believe they serve the same purpose as our angel of death, but they aren't bringing souls to heaven but to hell. This made my friend very concerned, but I assured him that he was a good person and that they must have been there for someone else. He wasn't convinced, and night after night, between midnight and 4 a.m., he would call me in a complete panic and inform me they were back again.

After about two weeks of this, a night went by when finally I didn't hear from him. The next morning I called his room, and to my relief he answered. I asked him how he was, and he explained he had finally got a full night of sleep, as the ghoul-men hadn't been circling the hallways the whole night the night before. He was no longer in fear and knew they weren't coming back. I asked how he knew this, and he said that the man in the room next to him, a man with the same first name who was about the same age as him, had passed away in the middle of the night the night before. These ghouls must have been trying to figure out which "Michael" they were there for and finally figured it out. I hope I am wrong about what these mysterious ghoulish-looking "men" were there for, for the sake of the now deceased other Michael. I'm pretty sure I'm not though, and I know I never want to get a visit or even just catch a glimpse of these figures personally.

43

THE DEMON IN THE CAR

A woman named Sally from Michigan was driving from work to pick up her son, Adam, from the babysitter's house. It was around eight p.m. when she finally arrived. She went to the door, and after exchanging pleasantries with the babysitter for a couple of minutes, she and her son were in the car on their way home. They arrived back at their house at around 8:45 p.m., and her son knew the routine and immediately ran up the stairs to change into his pajamas and get ready for bed. He was nine years old and knew the Friday night routine well.

After he was done brushing his teeth, he called his mom up to read him a story and tuck him in. By the time everything was done and Sally was finally ready for bed, it was almost midnight. As Sally lay in her bed trying to fall asleep, she began to hear what sounded like whispering coming from Adam's room. She thought she must be hearing things, but after a few minutes, she was sure she heard him. Knowing her son was probably underneath his blankets with a flashlight, one comic book or another in his hands, she went to his room and listened outside the door for a minute, and sure enough, he was whispering. She entered the room and saw him just as she had imagined he would be, under the covers and reading by flashlight. She halfheartedly admonished him but told him he needed to get some sleep and to put the book away and go to sleep. Adam did what he was told, and she tucked him back in. Sally went back to her room and fell right asleep.

Around three a.m. she awoke with a start to the sound of low giggling and more whispering coming from Adam's room. She looked at the clock and was angry that he was still awake reading his comic books and angrily stormed into his bedroom. She did this only to find her son sitting on the edge of his bed and looking into his closet. The closet door was wide open, and this was very unusual, as her son always kept that door closed. The hairs on the back of her neck stood up, and an overwhelming sense of fear and dread overtook her as she stared at her son, who was in turn staring, without blinking, into the closet. She tried to shake the feelings she was having and demanded to know what he was doing up at this time of night, and she also asked why he had been whispering and giggling at three in the morning. At first her son didn't answer, so she asked him again. More authority in her voice this time. When he still wouldn't answer her, or look away from the closet for that matter, she was suddenly concerned.

Sally rushed over to her son and put her arm around him and shook him gently. "Adam?" she asked. "Adam, are you okay?" After shaking him more aggressively over and over again and continuously asking if he was okay, finally he turned his head to look at her. His eyes were all black, and he responded, "Adam isn't here right now, but I'm Jack, and I can be your son if you'd like." Then he opened his mouth abnormally wide, like a snake that unhinges its jaw to devour an antelope. Sally says this was what she immediately thought of, a snake devouring its prey. Adam screamed as his mouth opened further and further, and as Sally fell backwards onto the floor, her son started to giggle very low at first, then maniacally and louder and louder. Sally had to do everything she could not to turn and run from the room, and she demanded that whatever had her son let him go and leave the house.

After about five minutes of reciting some prayers, Adam finally stopped laughing, blinked and fell onto his bed into a deep sleep. Sally couldn't immediately wake him and considered calling an ambulance, but what would she tell them? Her son seemed possessed by a demon, and once it left his body, she was having trouble waking him up? No, that wouldn't do at all. Sally sat the whole night at the foot of her son's bed, and when she woke up the next morning, everything was normal with Adam. He said he had no memory of the night before, but when she mentioned the name Jack, Adam shrugged and said, "That's the little boy who lives in Michelle's closet." Michelle was the little girl who was the daughter of his babysitter.

44

MORE SHADOW ENTITIES

My friend Rachel told me a story once of something that she had experienced when she was a little girl. She said every night for about two months, starting when she had just turned eight years old, when she went to bed, as soon as the lights were out, two dark shadow beings would suddenly appear in the corner of her room by her bedroom door. They would descend from the ceiling onto the floor at the foot of her bed and just stand there watching her. She would always immediately close her eyes when she saw them and try to pretend like she was sleeping. She said they would not only stand there and watch her pretend to sleep but also move around her room, sometimes lurking in the corners of the small bedroom and seeming to be communicating with each other. She said it was like they were two regular men having a conversation. Their shadowy arms would be moving, and their heads would turn and look at her at certain points.

What was even stranger was that she told me she could "hear" what they were saying in her head. It was like the whole conversation was taking place telepathically, and she could hear every word. She couldn't remember much of it the next day, and after a few months she had become so sleep deprived she started sleeping in her sister's room, and by the time she went back into her room, she never saw them again. When I asked her if she remembered any of what they were saying, she said that she vaguely remembers them talking about taking her to meet "the others" and when the right time would be. This absolutely terrified me due to my own frightening and perpetual experiences with shadow beings, but she said she tries not to think about it and never received a visit again.

45

DON'T ANSWER THEM

A friend of mine we will call David had a son who was four years old at the time he told me this story. His son's name was Rowan. While on a break at work one day, I noticed David wasn't his usual happy-go-lucky self and asked him what was up. He knew I was a psychic and said if it weren't for that fact, he wouldn't even talk about it for fear he would be looked at as "insane or something." He said Rowan had been having nightmares and almost every night for the past six months had been screaming for his dad to come and help him. David would go running into his son's room and find the boy terrified and shaking so badly he couldn't talk or even stand up. David would carry him into the master bedroom and let him spend the night in there with him and his wife. After a couple of months of this it just became commonplace, and the entire family was losing sleep over it, and nobody knew what to do about these "nightmares" that Rowan was having. Rowan couldn't or wouldn't articulate exactly what was going on in these nightmares. It seemed, however, that Rowan didn't see these occurrences as nightmares but as actual events taking place in his room almost every night. Kind of like a monster-in-the-closet type thing.

The night before this talk I was having with David at work was particularly stressful and terrifying for not only Rowan but David too. Rowan had woken up at the usual time, screaming and crying for his dad to come and help him. David ran down into Rowan's room, as he always did, but this time was something different. When he got to his son's room, he didn't find him terrified and crying, sitting up in his bed like usual. This time Rowan was sound asleep and couldn't have possibly been calling out to David. Confused, David went over and sat on the chair next to his son and ended up falling asleep there for the entire night.

The next morning when Rowan had woken up and saw his dad sleeping next to his bed in the chair, he asked him what he was doing. David, not wanting to scare his already stressed out and petrified son, told him he just wanted to sleep in his room to be close to him because he loved him and had gotten so used to Rowan sleeping in his bed with him. This answer seemed to satisfy the young toddler, and they went into the kitchen to have breakfast before the sitter arrived and David went off to work for the day. As they were eating though, Rowan looked up at his father and said, "They called you, didn't they, Daddy? When they call you, you aren't supposed to let them know you heard them." David decided not to respond and went to work as usual. That was what he told me the reason was for his awkward and seemingly scared behavior at work that day.

46

PHONE CALL FROM HELL

J oseph and Bill had been best friends ever since middle school when Bill had moved into the neighborhood and into the house next door to Joseph. They were the same age and almost had the exact same birthday as well. This close friendship extended to the boys' families as well, with their parents being super close and their sisters as well. Now that they were in high school and driving, they did even more together, and there wasn't usually a time when you would see one without the other. Bill was a bit wilder than Joseph and gained a reputation as "trouble" in their high school, but that didn't bother Joseph 'cause he figured he knew his best friend, who he now considered a brother, better than anyone else.

Unfortunately a tragedy took place that brought the families even closer together. What happened to Joseph afterwards, though, was something altogether terrifying. Bill had wanted to go to a party one Saturday night, and though Joseph wanted to go with him, his grandfather was visiting, and his mother had asked him to stay in and spend some time with him. His grandfather was ailing, and she thought they may not get many more chances to see him. Bill decided to go alone, and Joseph begged him not to, knowing he was always the designated driver and that Bill would be drinking and had no willpower to say no to drugs and alcohol. However, Bill wouldn't change his mind, and Joseph was helpless to stop him. Joseph made Bill promise that no matter what time it was, he would call him if he needed a ride home and that he wouldn't drink and drive. Bill laughed but promised his best friend this one thing.

Sure enough, at exactly 3:30 in the morning Joseph received a call from Bill's cell phone. He was woken up by the ringing of the familiar ringtone he had designated for his best friend. When he answered the phone, however, he was surprised that Bill didn't sound drunk at all and wasn't even asking for a ride home. Bill instead sounded absolutely terrified and was screaming into the phone to Joseph. He was saying things that made no sense like, "Help me! They're coming for me!" and, "Joseph, please, I need you!" As Joseph tried to get a word in edgewise, which he had been completely unsuccessful due to the absolutely horrific yelling and begging of his best friend, Joseph jumped out of bed and started to get dressed, all the while yelling over Bill's pleas and trying to ask where he was. All of a sudden, Joseph heard a loud and deep, demonic-sounding growl, and then Bill yelled, "NO!" and the call was disconnected.

In an absolute panic, Joseph ran into his mom's room and frantically told her what had just happened with the phone call from Bill. Concerned, his mother decided it would be best to call Bill's mother, they were best friends too, after all, and if something was wrong with Bill, she knew his mother would want to know. Bill's mother picked up on the second ring and was hysterically crying into the phone before Joseph's mother even said a word. All Joseph's mother could make out was that something bad had happened to Bill that night.

Joseph and his mother rushed next door to see what was

going on, and when they went inside, there were a couple of police officers in the house. It turned out Bill had died in a car crash, most likely while driving under the influence of alcohol and/or drugs, and his car had hit the middle divider on the highway doing eighty miles per hour. He was not wearing his seatbelt and was ejected from the vehicle through the front windshield. This was when Joseph told everyone about the phone call he had just received from Bill and explained that was the reason why he and his mother had come over to see what was going on. The one officer told him that what he was saying was impossible, as they had shown up to the scene of Bill's accident at no later than 2:00 in the morning. The phone call he made to Joseph from his cell phone would have been an hour and a half later, and Bill was already pronounced deceased, and his cell phone smashed to bits from the crash.

47

THE BALLOON

I was at a birthday party recently for a little girl named Leonia. Leonia was turning three, and because she was one of the few toddlers in the neighborhood, when my two-and-a-half-year-old son was invited to her party, I was thrilled for him. My husband and I don't have much family, and the family we do have, nobody has small children.

My son and I were at the house, and there were about fifteen toddlers running around in the living room, trying their best to make friends with each other and play some games with the balloons. The adults, myself included, were in the adjacent kitchen. We could see the whole living room from where we were in the kitchen and were keeping an eye on the kids while also preparing the snacks we were going to serve to them in just a few minutes.

Suddenly I heard an audible gasp out of one of the other mothers. I guess I wasn't the only one who heard this because all of us moms turned to look at what this now freaked-out-looking mom was looking at that made her gasp this way. There were balloons with weights on them all over the living room, in all different colors. If there weren't weights on them, the helium would have made them float to the ceiling, which was too high for us to have retrieved them without a ladder. One of the balloons was off the floor, floating there in midair! This was spectacular in and of itself because, as I already said, there were weights on the balloons, and therefore they couldn't float. If a weight had come off any of the balloons, it would just float high up to the ceiling. So someone or something had to be holding this balloon. We couldn't believe our eyes as we watched this one balloon move through the living room until it stopped right behind Leonia, the birthday girl. She turned around, saw the balloon, took it in her hand and said, "Thank you," and then giggled and turned away to play.

I said my goodbyes and grabbed my son and left. It wasn't so much the balloon thing that freaked me out so bad or shook me up so much. I am a psychic, so I saw something nobody else did, nobody except possibly Leonia. I saw what was making the balloon act in such a seemingly bizarre way. There, holding the balloon, was the ghostly figure of a man. He was wearing a suit and a top hat, and after he handed the balloon to the little girl, he turned to me and smiled. It was a sickening grin of razor-sharp, green and yellow teeth. He then licked his lips and winked at me before disappearing into a dark corner of the living room. I decided not to tell Leonia's parents what I had seen. My son already has trouble making friends, so I just told them the balloon made me scared and laughed with them about how silly I had been.

I don't let my son go over there to play without me, and I will never let him spend the night or go anywhere near that property without me there to protect and watch over him. One day I will talk to Leonia's mom, but I should probably get to know her a little better, as my son really does love playing with her daughter.

48

MY GUARDIAN ANGEL

When I was a little girl, somewhere around the age of nine or ten years old, I was in a really bad car wreck with my father and stepmother. We were driving back from one holiday celebration or another at my uncle's house and had to take the highway in order to get home. My baby sister was in the car too; she was only an infant of about six months old or so. I will tell the story to the best of my memory, as no matter how hard I try, I can't recall all of the details.

I remember driving along the highway, and everything was fine. I was sitting in the back seat with my little sister in the car seat next to me. Out of nowhere I had a terrible feeling and started begging my father to switch seats with me and let me sit in the front. I was crying and clawing on his shirt. After about ten minutes of this, much to my stepmother's annoyance, my father finally gave in and sat me in the front with my seat belt on, and he went into the back seat with my baby sister. My stepmother was driving.

A few minutes later, I looked up from whatever I was doing and saw a car spinning out of control. It was just going around and around and moving through each of the four lanes of the highway right in front of us. I remember feeling my father's hand on my left shoulder and bracing for impact. Sure enough, we smashed right into this car. I had my seatbelt on but must have been very confused or passed out or something 'cause the next thing I remember I was unbuckling my seat belt and opening the passenger-side door and wandering out of the car.

Luckily we were somehow on the shoulder of the highway, and there were some dense trees there where I had gotten out. I wasn't awake for long enough to take more than two steps, and this part I remember very clearly, or so I think I do. When I woke up again, I was being carried by what seemed like a man's arms, and I assumed it was my dad, and I started to whimper and snuggled into him, keeping my eyes closed the whole time. Then, suddenly I got one of those feelings I always got when something wasn't right and like something bad was about to happen. Only, nothing did. Well, not really. I looked up and saw who or what was carrying me out of those woods. It was some sort of humanoid figure; it was wearing a hooded sweatshirt with the hood up over a baseball cap. The man seemed to be trying very hard not to allow me to see his face. He sat me back in the car, and I saw him go around to check the pulse of my dad, who was lying on the floor in the back seat, and my step-mother, whose airbag had deployed and knocked her out. He seemed satisfied and then went to the back and handed my fussing baby sister her pacifier. He then knelt next to me until the police arrived.

I must have fallen asleep yet again because the next thing I remember is the police and ambulances arriving and bringing all of us to the hospital. Everyone in my family was okay, and we all recovered pretty quickly and moved on, but I never forgot the man who saved me.

Later on I got curious and asked my dad about what had

happened that night, and he said he didn't remember much except for seeing the car and then putting one hand on me and one hand on my sister's car seat. He explained, and I never knew this, that the back seat of the old, beat-up car we were driving was detached, and if it weren't for him being in the back seat, my sister could have gone, car seat and all, through the windshield. It was the early '90s, what can I say? The seatbelt was just for show, extremely dangerous I know, but because the seat detached and was broken, she would have gone flying forward on impact had my father's body not been blocking her.

He showed me pictures of the accident from the newspaper, and I saw, to my horror and surprise, that the person who saved me that night was the man who was spinning out of control in the middle of the highway. He was twenty-one years old, and his name was Raymond. He had had a medical emergency while driving and lost control of the vehicle. Unfortunately he didn't survive the impact. I am fully convinced his spirit saved my life, as I had a concussion and must have wandered into the woods without knowing what I was doing. He had stayed with me until the police came and must have crossed over 'cause I never saw him again. I never told my father about the man because he didn't like when I would speak about my abilities or visitations and still to this day doesn't like or understand it when I do. I knew that something was "off" or different about this man who was carrying me; I was just too out of it to be able to put my finger on it.

49
EVIL ANGEL

When I was twenty-three years old, I was out one night drinking and singing karaoke and had had a bit too much to drink. I called my boyfriend at the time and asked if he would take a cab to the bar so he could drive me and my truck home. He didn't have a license, but knew how to drive, and I knew it would be better than me possibly hurting someone or getting in trouble with the law. He agreed and was there about twenty minutes later. My house was about fifteen long blocks away from the bar.

We got in my truck and started to drive. I was blasting music and having a grand old time when suddenly he said to me, "Put your seatbelt on, now!" I did what I was told and attempted to buckle my seat belt. However, as I turned to fasten the metal piece in to secure the belt, the airbag suddenly deployed. The next thing I remember was waking up on the ground inside a local park. I couldn't move and had this terrifying thought that I might be paralyzed. I tried with all of my might and strength to get back to the car to check on my boyfriend, but I simply couldn't do it.

As I lay there, I closed my eyes and suddenly had the feeling like I was floating or possibly even being carried. I wasn't wearing a jacket, and it was nighttime and winter in north-eastern Pennsylvania. I must've passed out. The next thing I remember I was lying next to the truck, which wasn't possible because I couldn't move from the waist down and had been at least twenty feet away before I had had the strange floating sensation. I also remember being really warm. I started screaming for my boyfriend, but he was nowhere to be seen. I was all alone and terrified of what could have happened to him.

I also remember the revelation coming upon me that one of my Spirit guides must have somehow moved me closer to the vehicle so it would be easier for the police and paramedics to find me. No sooner had I had this thought and also let out a short prayer of thanks than a low and deep voice responded, "You're welcome, and now you owe me. Or maybe Charles would like to pay us back? He's not as protected." It was ominous and put a chill right through me, and drunk or not, I knew it wasn't the voice of any of my guides or that of any angel I had ever encountered.

It turned out I had shattered my pelvis, or the airbag did because of my awkward, turned position when it deployed. My boyfriend, I would find out later, was more drunk than I was and had slammed his head against the steering wheel because the airbag didn't deploy.

It's been about fifteen years since that accident, and shortly after it happened, the doctors said it was due to a head injury he received, which I know was most likely caused by that crash that night, Charles started to go a little crazy. He became violent, abusive and paranoid. This was nowhere near what he was like before the accident. He insisted the television was talking to him and that he was seeing strange, dark figures in the night telling him to kill me and then himself. I eventually left Charles but found out recently that he had died two years ago, at the age of thirty-four, from a brain aneurysm. I always wondered if that evil voice had anything to do with it.

50

THE DARK MAN

This story has a lot to do with the last one I just related here. I have a three-and-a-half-year-old son who, about a year ago, started being scared to be alone in the house. When he was alone, whether he was playing, sleeping or watching his cartoons, he would always end up screaming and running out of whatever room he was in. He would be crying and telling me there was a "Dark Man" in the room with him who was pinching him. This gave me great cause for alarm. As a psychic myself, this is the exact sort of thing that happened to me at his age, according to my parents, when I first started to receive visitations from the other side. I don't know who or what was haunting me when I was little, but I was worried for my son.

One day when he was playing alone in his room, I decided to listen in. I heard him giggling and laughing and having a great time by himself. He was also having a conversation in toddler talk with something I couldn't see. I breathed a sigh of relief and went on about my day. No more than two minutes after I moved away from my son's bedroom door did he come running out as fast as his little legs could carry him, screaming and crying about "the Dark Man."

I didn't leave my son alone in the house again and did everything within my power to rid my house and my son of this haunting. To rid us of this evil presence known now as the dark man. Nothing was working, and I was out of ideas.

One day I was interviewing a psychic online for one of my shows on YouTube, and I mentioned what was going on with my son. She then began to describe Charles to a tee. Right down to the whiteness of his teeth (he became obsessed with teeth whitening after the accident) and larger than normal ears. She then said the name Charles and told me that this entity was a soul who was scared to pass on and was connected to me somehow. She said he would play nice with my son, and once my son was laughing and smiling and having a good time, he would turn on him and scare him by changing his face to make it look evil or even pinching him. He was purposely shielding himself from me, knowing probably that I could get rid of him. Charles had become extremely abusive in life, which was why I left him, and then he decided to torment a child I had with my now husband. Most likely out of sheer jealousy.

I called in some friends from the psychic and Wiccan communities, and we were eventually able to cross Charles over. My son no longer fears "the Dark Man" and isn't afraid anymore to be alone in his bedroom. I know Charles crossed over because ever since we did the blessing and charm on my son and my house, it's been infested with ladybugs. This was how Charles always told me he would appear to me from the other side and let me know he was with me. I'm glad his soul is at peace but am still angry he took it all out on my innocent toddler.

51

THE WARNING

J asmine was seventeen when she told me her story. She said her aunt had died suddenly when she was just a kid, and it was the first time she had had to deal with death. It was her mother's older sister who had passed, and her entire family was just grief stricken.

Jasmine said she was young enough that she didn't remember much about her aunt except she was terrified, seemingly for no reason, of her uncle Alexander. He was gruff and had a beard, but he had never done anything threatening towards Jasmine, but something about him just gave her the creeps. It turned out her uncle had slowly poisoned her aunt and had fled the house, so when Jasmine's aunt was found, Alexander was nowhere around. He must have known what he had done would eventually be figured out, so when her aunt finally passed on, he didn't want to be around to be arrested and held accountable. Everyone had assumed he had gone back to his home country, and tried to move along as best they could.

It was about six months later when Jasmine started having strange dreams about her aunt. In these dreams, or she would sometimes call them nightmares, Jasmine would see her aunt in the mirror in her bathroom, and her aunt would have red eyes and be yelling nonsense at her. She would jump up and run into her parents' bedroom to sleep. She simply told her parents she had had a bad dream but didn't go into detail for fear of upsetting her "overly superstitious" mother, as she put it.

One night Jasmine had another nightmare about her aunt, but this time she could understand her aunt, again appearing to her in the bathroom mirror in the dream, telling her to wake up her parents immediately. Jasmine, who knew she was dreaming, asked how she would do that. Her aunt's eyes then turned glowing red, and she reached through the mirror and screamed, "WAKE THEM UP NOW!"

Jasmine jumped up and ran into her parents' bedroom, again pleading with them to stay for the night so she didn't have to be in her room alone. Her parents were agitated that their daughter, who was almost eleven years old, was sleeping in their bed almost every night. Her father insisted she go back into her room but told her he would walk her there and make sure everything was safe. As he searched Jasmine's room for monsters in the closet and under the bed, Jasmine just stood there shaking and crying and begging not to have to stay in that room alone.

Her bedroom was on the first floor of the house, and as he was standing from looking under her bed, her father suddenly stopped and put his finger to his lips to silence her. That was when they both heard the distinct sound of someone trying to break in. Her father had seen a silhouette outside her bedroom window out of the corner of his eye when he stood up. He called the police, and when they arrived, there was someone trying to break into their house. The man had a bag with him that contained duct tape, a gun, several knives and handcuffs. What he was planning to do with these items can only be left to the imagination, as, thankfully, he was carted off to jail, and Jasmine never knew what became of him.

I'm confused to this day as to why Jasmine's aunt chose to help the family out in such a horrific and evil way, by terrifying her niece for months the way she did. Jasmine was still having the same nightmare about her aunt six years later when she told me this story. I wonder if it's because Alexander disappeared and was never seen again. He never had to face justice or be accountable for what he had done or answer the family's many questions as to why he had done it. Rumor has it he went back to his native country and died of a drug overdose, but nobody is sure.

52

RESURRECTION MARY

In Justice, Illinois, there is a long stretch of road where there is a cemetery called Resurrection Cemetery almost smack-dab in the middle. While we should all know by now the dangers that accompany the act of hitchhiking, it was very common back in the day, and even now, there is one Spirit who seems to get picked up quite a bit.

Legend has it that while driving down this road after the sun goes down, you may come across a very attractive young woman with her thumb out seeming to be in need of a ride somewhere. Being attractive as she is, she is said to mainly attract men who will pull over and allow her access into their vehicles by offering her a ride. The girl doesn't speak much and comes off as a bit rude to some who have claimed to have seen her. It's also reported a lot that the temperature in the car goes down a few degrees upon her entering it. Once the driver reaches her destination though, she steps out of the vehicle and disappears into thin air.

There is another variation to this legend that says the girl will enter the vehicle and tell the driver where she would like to go. She tells him as well that her name is Mary and a little bit about her life. While she seems a bit awkward and is dressed strangely for the times, she is otherwise quite pleasant and seemingly well read. Upon reaching her destination, she gets out and closes the door with a smile and a "thanks" and even turns to wave the driver off as she walks up the stairs to her home. Upon discovering she has left either a hat or a scarf (or some other random article of clothing or other property depending on who is telling the story), the driver returns to the home the next day and knocks on the door. An elderly woman resembling Mary answers the door, and the driver then explains he had given her a ride the night before and had dropped her off at that house and that she had left whatever the item was in the car. The woman then exclaims in shock, "Mary is my daughter, and she died years ago!" Letting the driver know he had actually given a ride to a hitchhiking ghost.

53

A GROUP HALLUCINATION?

I was a wilderness supervisor in the Arizona desert. I was camping every single night; because of my job, I kind of lived like that—just drifting through the woods. As time went on, I figured I was used to all of the strange and even the normal sounds in and of the woods.

One night, near Aravaipa Canyon, a couple of my buddies came out to camp with me. The night was quiet but not very peaceful. It was a very weird kind of quiet, the kind that makes you feel there is something around that has scared everything else off. Despite my good friends being there, I couldn't shake the feeling of dread and terror that kept creeping up inside me. I kept my composure, as my friends seemed as though they didn't realize something was amiss.

Eventually we put our fire out and set up to go to sleep for the night. Just as I started to fall asleep, my hair was suddenly pulled, and I was half dragged out of my sleeping bag. At the exact same time that I managed to pull away and jump up onto my feet, both of my friends had done the same. All three of us were out of breath and staring wide eyed at each other, wondering what in the world just happened. We brushed ourselves off and finally convinced each other, somehow, that we had all had the same very real-feeling dream all at the same time. Nothing else ever happened to me, not that night or ever again, but I still get the chills when I think about it.

54

SCREAMING APPARITION

A friend of mine works for the US Forest Service and has seen some pretty strange things throughout his tenure. One night we were camping, and I asked him to tell me the most bizarre thing he had ever encountered while out on the job. He said that in 2006 in Hell's Canyon in Idaho, he was supervising a crew who were going to be working a straight-through twenty-four-hour shift. Because my friend was heading the crew that day, it was his job to go out on his ATV and scout the area. I'm still not sure exactly what the job was or what they were doing, but that isn't really important to the story.

He eventually found himself riding down an old logging road that hadn't been traveled in quite some time. It was extremely dangerous, and to make matters even worse, he explained a bobcat seemed to come out of nowhere and ended up smack-dab in the middle of the road, directly in his path. There was nowhere for him to go, as all to the sides of him were extremely rough and impossible to navigate brush and plant life. He managed to stop just short of the wild animal, and for about ten-seconds the two just stared at each other. All of a sudden, the cat let out a massive and extremely terrifying scream. Then, without any warning, it turned and ran up a nearby tree. It was strange to say the least, but my friend was just relieved to have the animal out of his way so he could continue scouting the land. I've seen other stories with similar encounters with wild cats and cabins and such, but my friend isn't into the paranormal and was aware of no such occurrences.

He quickly went on his way, and not long after something eerily similar yet distinctively different happened. This time though, it was a Native-looking woman who had suddenly appeared directly in front of him in the middle of the road. My friend said he swerved so as not to hit her and went headfirst over the handlebars of his ATV. When he finally got himself together and stood up to go and get back on his ride, he turned around and was face-to-face, within an inch away, with the random woman. She opened her mouth and let out the exact same scream the cat had let out just moments before. It was animalistic and violent sounding. She turned and ran off into the wilderness, and my friend booked it out of there and never looked back. Later on he learned of the legends of the skin-walkers all around in that area he was surveying.

55

LITTLE BLUE BOY

This is a story I keep hearing people tell me about a news article that happened somewhere in the southern United States in 2021. A mother was driving down a rural and desolate road with her three-year-old son when suddenly the little boy insisted she stop the car. He was screaming and carrying on so much the woman thought he was about to have an accident in his pants. They were in the middle of potty training, after all, so, mainly to humor him, his mom pulled over.

She very quickly realized though there was something much more serious than a potty accident happening. Her son was in a complete panic, crying almost to the point of hyperventilating. She jumped out of the car and quickly pulled him out as well. Holding him close, she asked what was wrong. He explained to her that there was a little boy on the side of the road, about his age, and that he was blue. The mother thought maybe her son was saying the boy was sad, and also she assumed this was just another one of her son's very vivid imaginary friend stories. The boy was an only child without much family around, and sometimes he made up very detailed lives for a whole bunch of "friends" he would talk to and play with regularly.

She tried assuring him it would be okay and coaxing him back into his car seat, but the boy would not budge. He insisted to his mother he had seen a blue boy and that he told him he is somewhere in the woods running all along the side of the road. He even told her exactly where the boy said he would be located. Underneath the smallest oak tree, a quarter of a mile up from the river. The blue boy also said his mommy was in the river, in her car. They had crashed.

The mother at this point was not only extremely concerned for her son, who was by the minute becoming more agitated and insistent she go and look for this boy, but also she was getting creeped out. She decided the best course of action would be to call the local police and report what had happened. Though reluctant, they finally decided to come out and check the woods, and they did find a little boy and his mother in the river. She was trapped in their car. The mother must have had a medical emergency and went off the road and into the water. The little boy somehow got out and tried to walk and get help but was overcome by the elements and didn't make it very far. Did this little boy really see the ghost of another little boy, and had he chosen a three-year-old like him because it would be more believable? We may never know, but what an amazingly creepy story.

56

SHE CAME HOME

Pete was a plasterer living in Northumberland, England. He made a pretty good living and was self-employed. One day he was doing some work at a quaint little cottage not too far from his house. The owners had just moved in, so Pete wasn't familiar with them at all. As far as he could tell, there was a mom and a dad and one teenage daughter. He hadn't met the daughter yet, but the mom and dad were extremely nice people.

On his third day of working there, the father was out, and the mom was on her way to do some grocery shopping. She told Pete that her daughter, named Rachel, should be home any minute and to please just introduce himself so she wasn't worried and to also please tell her she was just running to the store and would be back within the hour to start dinner. Pete said okay, and off she went.

About fifteen minutes later, Pete heard what sounded like a young woman crying coming from one of the back bedrooms. The cottage was quite small, so he knew what he was hearing with no mistake, and also he knew where it was coming from.

He went and knocked on the door where the sobbing was coming from and heard the gentle and sniffling, quite upset voice of a young girl inside saying, "Come in." Pete opened the door and peeked into the room. He introduced himself and told the young girl her mom would be home within the hour. He said, "You must be Rachel." The young girl started sobbing even harder now and said, "No! I'm Julia! They left and tried to leave me behind. Shut my door and leave me alone!" Pete did as he was told.

He was now extremely uncomfortable and just wanted the mom to come back so she could console her daughter and perhaps make the situation less awkward for all involved. The sobbing grew louder and louder as the minutes passed, but when the girls' mother pulled into the driveway, it stopped altogether. "Thank goodness for small favors," said Pete to himself.

When the mother came through the door, she immediately asked if Rachel had come home yet. Pete explained that while Rachel hadn't come home yet, her other daughter, Julia, had and that she was very upset and sobbing in the back bedroom. The mother gasped and dropped her groceries all over the floor. "How do you know about Julia?" she asked. Pete explained again that she was in the back bedroom and crying about being left behind by someone. The mother explained to Pete that their oldest daughter, Julia, had died in a violent car crash a year before, and the family had bought the cottage and moved across the country with the hopes of getting a fresh start. When she ran to the back bedroom, of course no one was there, but there was a slight indentation on the bed where Pete had seen her sitting just moments ago.

Pete finished his work on the house a few weeks later and never spoke of the encounter again with the residents. It seemed like it was too painful for them, and he was extremely happy to be done and to move on himself, to working in a much less haunted house.

57

THE EYES

I remember when I was five or six years old living in one apartment or another in my hometown of Paterson, New Jersey. We lived on the second floor of a three-story house. My sister, who was four years older than me, would often go and stay at one of our many cousins' houses for the night, and I was always left alone with my parents during those times.

One weekend when my sister was gone, I was playing in our shared room, and it seemed as soon as darkness fell, this overwhelming sense of creepiness came over me. This happened often but never to this degree, not at that point in my life anyway. I still get the chills just thinking about it. At around 9 p.m. my dad came in and tucked me in for bed, and despite this sense of fear and dread, I fell asleep fairly quickly.

I woke suddenly and with a start in the middle of the night and for some reason was immediately drawn to the only window in the small bedroom. I immediately turned to look and saw a pair of glowing red and somehow evil-looking eyes staring back at me. Remember, we were on the second floor, and there was no balcony or fire escape or any possible way that anyone could be looking into that particular window. I was frozen in fear. I couldn't scream or call out. The only thing I could think to do was cover myself, my face included, completely with the covers and close my eyes really tight. If I pretended like it wasn't there, maybe it wouldn't be. I don't know how long I lay there like that, but eventually I guess I fell back asleep.

The next night I was terrified of sleeping alone in my room, but it was another night at least until my sister was back home. My mom and dad gave me the usual parent answer of, "It was just a bad dream. There's no way anything could possibly be looking in your window." Needless to say, I didn't take much comfort in that. That night I finally fell asleep and woke up again in the middle of the night with a start, this time to two sets of glowing red and menacingly evil eyes staring back at me. Fed up with seeing things like this (I am a physical medium and have seen the grotesque, evil and the dead for as far back as I can remember), I yelled for it to go to hell and leave me alone. I also told it it didn't scare me at all. Before I could even get those last words out, the things, whatever they were, were suddenly transformed into gigantic shadow beings with "bodies" to go with the red eyes. There were two of them, and they started violently banging on my window, trying to get in. I tried to scream but realized I couldn't.

My father came charging into my room and turned the light on, asking me what in the world was going on. I explained, but he just thought I was lying and had been making the noises myself to try to get attention because I missed my sister and was angry she got to go away for the night and I didn't. This couldn't have been further from the truth, and he knew it, but because he couldn't explain it, I guess he was angry nonetheless. He saw how terrified I was, but it was like he couldn't allow himself to see it, and he told me to cut the bull and go to sleep.

I'll never forget my mother though, standing there at my bedroom door and looking from me to the window and then back again. She didn't say a word, but I knew she knew what it was and why it was after me. Come to think of it—I forgot until just now to ask her about it.

58

THE BLACK LINE

Violet was a twenty-seven-year-old mother of two young children who used to live down the street from me when I was a teenager. I would always see her pushing the stroller up the street and around the block with her two adorable little kids in it. Her son was four, and her daughter was about a year and a half when this happened. Violet and I would talk when she would pass by my house, and sometimes she would sit for a few minutes and just hang out. She always had bruises on her face and body, and being psychic, I knew without having to ask that they were coming from her violent, alcoholic husband, Bill. Also, we sometimes heard her screaming in the middle of the night when he would be in one of his rages.

One day after Violet came and sat with me on my front steps, pushing her kids in the stroller, all beat up and black and blue, I realized she had left her daughter's bottle there on my steps. I was on my way out when I saw it and decided I would return it when I got home later. It was around ten at night when I went and rang Violet's doorbell. I immediately heard the screaming and crying; Violet and her kids were being terrorized. I decided I would have the good sense to just leave the bottle there in front of the door so as not to have to face Bill and his drunken wrath myself. I also planned on maybe mentioning it the next time she came by. I was only a teenager, and it was fairly simple in my inexperienced head—"just leave him" I would tell her, and just like in the movies, she would live happily ever after, and Bill would get hit by a semi or something.

As I turned to walk away, though, Bill opened the door. "What do YOU want?" he asked. I explained I was just returning the bottle Violet had left on the steps earlier. I could see behind him, and Violet and the kids were cowering in one corner of the small kitchen. Bill grabbed me by my arm and pulled me into the kitchen, and I fell to the floor. I don't know what horrible fate might have befallen me had what happened next not done so. All of a sudden Bill was lifted about ten feet into the air and thrown into the wall on the opposite side of the kitchen Violet, her kids and now myself were on. As we all watched in horror and shock, Bill got up and started to charge towards us again, bloody and bruised as he now was from hitting the wall as hard as he did. Well, he was thrown back into the wall yet again. Before he got back to his feet, we all watched as a black line started on the floor and went directly between where the four of us were and where Bill now was. It even went up to the ceiling. It was almost as if something had intervened and was daring Bill to cross this line.

As he sat there, just as we did, in shock and awe staring at what was happening, an extremely dark black blob of a shadow floated slowly up out of Bill's stomach and into the ceiling. I ran over to Violet and the kids, and by the time we had remembered about him and looked over at the now messed-up wall, Bill was gone. I'm not sure what ever happened to him, but I speak to Violet on Facebook now and then, and she is happily married to someone who is not Bill, with four kids. Her oldest two are in college. I've had the good sense not to ask about Bill, and she never mentioned him or that night.

59

SHE WAS THE GHOST

Janine, her husband Jonathan and their two teenage kids moved into a new house on a very rural and very old farm in South Dakota in 2004. From the moment they stepped foot on the property, something seemed off. They always felt like they were being watched, but the presence or whatever it was seemed benign, almost curious in nature.

One night as Janine stood up to put another log on the fire, while she was all alone in the living room, she swears this is what happened next. She told me she was suddenly super dizzy and actually had to lean forward against the mantel of the fireplace to catch herself. Once she finally felt composed enough to go and join her family in the other room for dinner, she turned around to make her way to the kitchen, where they were all gathered and waiting for her.

Her seventeen-year-old daughter was entering the living room as soon as Janine turned around, and they both saw the exact same thing. Suddenly there was a big table in the middle of the room, and a woman was serving some sort of meal out of a huge cauldron-looking thing. Sat at this table were two grown men, one young boy and one even younger girl. The woman seemed to notice Janine and kept staring at her while also trying to pretend like she wasn't seeing her. It seemed as though this mystery woman was scared and also trying to keep it together just as Janine was at the same time. The people were dressed in clothing from the late 1700s, and the woman was yelling for everyone to settle down for the meal's prayer.

The little boy suddenly looked over and, seeming to have also seen Janine just standing there staring in shock at the picture before her, tapped the older man next to him on the shoulder. He proceeded to whisper in the older man's ear and point back at Janine. The older man then turned to Janine and whispered something back to the boy. It was at this point that the woman took her place at the table, the little girl giggled and waved at Janine, and the entire scene suddenly disappeared, and Janine and her daughter were left standing there staring wide eyed at each other. They agreed not to tell the others in the family and to try to behave as normally as possible during dinner that night.

It's often said, and I fully believe, that time is not linear. All other lives, including so-called "past lives," are being lived by other versions of ourselves right now. This includes other present and future lives as well. Could this have just been a random time slip? Was the little boy and his mother from this "past" scene each thinking they were the ones seeing some sort of benign ghostly apparition? Maybe one day we will have these answers.

60

BUDDY

Recently, in the first three months of this year, I lost two very special people to me within three weeks of each other. One was a close friend of twenty-eight years and with whom I have a seventeen-year-old son, and the other was my stepfather, who had been with my mother for almost thirty-three years and who had raised me for most of the latter part of my minor life. They died in January and February respectively.

I've spoken before about my three-year-old son and his abilities and the fact that I worry about the things he sees sometimes because he doesn't know yet how to protect himself, and he definitely isn't old enough for me to teach him yet. My stepfather and my toddler were very close. They were best buddies, and that's exactly what we would call them. That's also what they would call each other, "Buddy." My son doesn't understand yet what it actually means when someone dies, so we all decided the best thing for now was to tell him my stepfather is in the hospital with the doctors because he is sick and ready to go to live with Jesus.

I recently got up the courage to transfer some of my stepdad's ashes into a very small container to put on my mantel at home. I stayed with my toddler at my mom's house when Gary, my stepdad, died back in February, and I was there for about two months before coming home. I brought the ashes with me, placed them on my altar surrounded by some crystals and gemstones, and moved on. I should explain that my seventeen-year-old son's father's name was Jeff, and he and I had been close friends even after our breakup and remained that way up until he passed suddenly, from an overdose, at the end of January.

About a week ago I noticed my toddler was playing alone in his bedroom almost all day long, when before we went to my mom's, he wouldn't step foot in there without me. I often hear him laughing and talking and giggling, and when I go in and ask whom he is talking to, he looks at the wall and giggles and then puts his finger to his mouth as if he's keeping in a big secret. Just the other day he walked past my altar and waved and said, "Hey, Buddy, let's go play in my room." He had waved to my stepfather's tiny little container of ashes, which he couldn't possibly have known was there.

About an hour ago from when I am writing this, he was on his fake cell phone talking, and when I asked whom he was speaking to, he told me it was his new friend, "Jeff." I almost fell over. There's no possible way he could have known about my ex passing or even anything about him, including his name. My seventeen-year-old was raised by my mother and stepfather and was just himself getting to know Jeff, his biological father, when he died four months ago. It's comforting, and I'll admit I'm a bit jealous I haven't received a visitation yet, but it makes me feel good knowing that my son has his best buddy, and mine, watching over and playing with him on a daily basis.

61

IT WANTED THE BABY

Alexis and Jeremy were twenty-seven years old in 2019 when they got married and bought their first home together. After dating for six years, they tied the knot and were trying to start their family. They even bought a house with this dream in mind. It had an extra room where they were going to put the baby's nursery. Within three months Alexis was expecting, and things went the way they usually do from that point on, and approximately nine months later, they welcomed their little boy, Jeremy Jr., into the world.

The baby was absolutely perfect and healthy, and the parents couldn't have been more joyful or proud. That is, until immediately upon bringing Jr. home from the hospital, when all of the strange things started to happen in their house. Started to happen, more accurately, in his nursery. It started with little things that could easily be chalked up to overtired and therefore forgetful parents. Drawers were opened when mom or dad were sure they had closed them. The night light was turned off when Jeremy Sr. was positive he had left it on for the little guy. Some of the things happening even started small arguments between the couple, and they finally decided they needed a break and maybe some sleep.

Alexis called her mother and asked her to come and help with Jr. for a few weeks. Her mother was delighted and took the trip across the country to come and help out. It wasn't long before her mother, Heather, also started noticing some very strange activity going on in the baby's room though. Most of it could be shaken off, but when she started hearing strange sounds coming from the baby monitor on a regular basis, she knew there was something very wrong. Every time she would put little Jeremy down to sleep and leave the room, she would hear strange and unintelligible whispers and even growling sounds coming from the monitor. She would run back into the room to find the baby sleeping soundly in his crib and nothing sinister going on at all. It was enough to make everyone think they were losing their minds.

They decided a camera for the baby's room would be a good investment, and they thought maybe it would help ease some of their fears and anxieties because now they would be able to see exactly what was going on in the room at any given time. At night was the worst when the noises would start coming through the monitor from the baby's room. Alexis would rush to where the camera monitor was in the kitchen, but she didn't see anything, until one night.

One night the growling and giggling and whispering coming from the nursery had become too much, and Alexis took little Jeremy and moved him into her room and placed his bassinet at the foot of her bed. Jeremy Sr. was gone for a week on a business trip, and her mom was staying in the guest room down the hall. Alexis got up to get a drink of water and just happened to glance at the monitor in the kitchen, which showed the cameras that were placed in both her room and Jeremy Jr.'s. She was so shocked she dropped her glass and ran over the broken pieces, cutting her foot along the way to get to her son.

She later explained what she had seen. There was a gigantic shadow figure, a huge humanoid all black and wearing some sort of cloak, eyes glowing red, standing over Jeremy's empty crib. Then at the same time in her room, another shadow entity that looked exactly like the one in his room was looming over the bassinet, and the baby was levitating out of it and seemingly into this thing's arms. As she ran, holding the audio monitor and tracking blood from her foot the whole way, she heard, "We are here for this baby!"

Nobody knows what really happened to little Jeremy, but this is the story Alexis insists on as she sits awaiting trial. She was accused of doing something to her son, as people, babies included, don't just vanish into thin air. According to most people, though we in this community know better, they also don't end up being kidnapped by cloaked shadow entities with glowing red eyes in the middle of the night either... Or do they?

62

MISS BARBARA

When I was in my early twenties and would party a lot, it was hard for me to hold down an apartment, and eventually I had nowhere to go. My friend Donna was gracious enough to take me into her small one bedroom, and I slept on the couch. I got a job immediately after moving in with her, and it was, thankfully, only two blocks away. It was at a diner, and being the new girl, I got the 4 p.m. to 4 a.m. shift right from the start.

Donna was away a lot to where we call in Jersey "down the shore," which really just means at the beach. Her girlfriend lived there, and that was where she spent most of her time. It was mostly just me and her ornery and very "bitey" cat named Lily in the apartment.

The building was old and had one of those old-fashioned elevators from like the 1950s, and it was constantly out of service. We lived on the sixth floor, and after working the twelve-hour shifts until four in the morning and then the hour of cleanup that comes with being a good waitress, I wouldn't walk through the front doors of the building until around 5 a.m. Sometimes it would be later if I decided to eat after my shift and side work was done. Whatever the time was, when I got back to the apartment building, it was still dark outside.

One night after about two weeks of living there and a week of working this ridiculous shift at the diner, I walked into the building and saw that the elevator was finally working. I hopped in and pressed the button to the sixth floor. The elevator didn't go up though and instead went down, taking me to the basement of this creepy, old building. I'm not gonna lie, back then I did everything I could to turn off my psychic abilities. Being a physical medium and not knowing what that really meant at the time was enough to make me wanna drink all the time—which I kind of did.

The elevator stopped in the basement, and the door opened up to let me out. I immediately felt the hairs on my arms and the back of my neck stand up and decided not to exit down there and to just go back up to the sixth floor. I was exhausted and in no mood for any spirits or their shenanigans. Furthermore I wasn't sure of any human element being down in that basement either. There were no apartments, but I had a feeling some of the area's homeless slept there on the cold, winter nights. I pressed the button for the sixth floor, and of course, the elevator didn't budge. I was stuck there in that creepy, old and probably rat-infested basement, and I was terrified. The only way to get out and up into my apartment was to walk through the darkness to the stairwell, and even then I had no idea where I was going. I didn't have a smartphone at the time, so there was no luxury of a flashlight either.

I exited the elevator and went to the left, moving completely on my intuition at this point and scared out of my wits. About a minute later I ran smack into an old woman. I screamed, and she just looked at me and laughed. She carried a flashlight and said, "Well, excuse me, young lady! I didn't see you there. Damn near startled me half to death!" and at this she chuckled a bit maniacally. Her teeth were almost all gone except for a few brown-stained pointy things that I guess you could consider teeth, and she and her breath smelled horrid. She asked me what I was doing, and I shakily explained about the elevator situation.

The old woman introduced herself as Miss Barbara and said she was a "kind of caretaker" in the building. She took me by the arm and led me to the exit door so I could get to the stairs. She looked around shiftily as I went to open the door, and grabbed my arm rather roughly. She looked me right in the eyes and said in an evil and malicious voice, "Don't ever come down here again! It's dangerous for someone so pretty as you to be lost in the dark down here. Never know what or who you might run into!" Then Barbara disappeared before my very eyes, and it was only then I realized she was a spirit.

Upon further research, I learned the original owner of that particular building had a wife named Barbara who used to take in the homeless way back when the building was first erected in the early 1900s. She was a kindly old woman, and when I looked at the picture, I knew it was the same woman. I went back down to the basement a couple more times after learning about the old woman and her humanitarian work because, being a physical medium, I knew I could help her pass on. I never saw her again, but when Donna came home and I told her about what had happened, she told me a part of the story I must've missed in my half-assed attempt to find out who this woman was.

It turns out that Barbara took in the wrong tenants, a young, homeless couple back in 1915, and after she gave them a room and a hot meal, they lured her to the basement by offering to help her go through the building and collect the trash from the hallways and bring it down there. Once they had her in the dark, they murdered her right there and took what little money she had on her. The two were never caught either.

I've visited Donna numerous times in the last year, almost thirteen years since my encounter with Barbara and ten years since I moved out of her apartment. The whole building has been remodeled, and Donna now has a basement apartment. Every time I walk through the now lit corridor to get to her front door, a part of me dreads and a part of me hopes that I will see Miss Barbara again.

63

THE TRICKSTERS

This is one that happened recently, in May of 2022. I livestream a lot on YouTube for my channel, and every Wednesday night I do a four-and-a-half-hour one-card oracle reading for anyone and everyone who comes along in the stream. It was hard to keep track of the list of people in the chat who wanted a reading and converse with the chat and channel and also give the messages to the people I was reading for. So I took on a helper. His name is Steven, and he and I also livestream on Tuesday night just to chat with everyone and catch up/unwind for the week ahead.

A few nights ago we were almost to the end of our almost five-hour stream when suddenly I gasped and told Steven that a "trickster" just walked out of his wall, to the left and right behind him. It possibly came from outside because there was a window right there behind him, and it looked a bit like the thing came out from behind the curtain. I didn't want to scare him, so I casually mentioned that a trickster was behind him, and it had bright, almost glowing, blue eyes. I realized afterwards there were three of them. They look like that old costume of a ghost where someone takes a white sheet, cuts two holes in it for eyes, and drapes it over a little kid. That was exactly what it looked like, only all black instead of white and like the blackness was draped over a very short toddler. Within minutes all hell broke loose, and Steven texted me explaining we needed to end the stream, as he had a huge bruise and burn mark randomly appear on his left arm. To the end of the stream you can see him silently praying as well.

I did some research. I've dealt with tricksters before, and almost one hundred percent of the time they are affiliated with some Native American tribe—but not these ones. These ones were demonic. Being a physical medium, I should have known this right away, but because I was channeling and paying attention to the messages coming through for my chat, I didn't understand what was happening at first. The fact he had two very small demons, one with glowing light blue eyes, wasn't even the strongest or scariest part for me. The third thing I saw definitely took the cake on that! It was something that was very curious about the trickster and making itself look like them because of this curiosity. It was an extraterrestrial. Of what kind I can't tell you because it was presenting to me as looking exactly like ET from the movie. The ET seemed playful and curious, while the tricksters were dangerous and scary.

The next day I expressed my concern to Steven and told him about what I had seen and what he needed to do in order to get rid of them. He had a terrible nightmare that night and tried to tell me about it but had suddenly forgotten most of it. There were marks on his wrists as though he had been tightly handcuffed, and my psychic senses told me he had actually been abducted and handcuffed to some sort of hospital bed. I am mailing him a care package with some spell jars and tar water, holy water and fresh sage to ward off the demons until I can get him further help. For the extraterrestrial, though, I have no idea what to do. I just hope the two demonic entities leave him alone because so far they seem to be heavily influencing other people in Steven's house to start to pick fights with him. Their usually gentle personalities have, in just three short days, become incredibly violent. I hope my care package arrives in time. All I can do is pray.

64

THE BARBECUE

Shannon was at a friend's house for a barbecue in the summer of 2016. She was quite nervous because she hadn't seen her friends Josiah and Kimber since the death of their four-year-old daughter in 2013. She just didn't know what to say to them. Shannon herself wasn't married and at thirty-two years old still wasn't even thinking about kids. She had been close to Chloe though, the little girl, and was even asked to be godmother to her. Chloe's death was so tragic, such a beautiful and bright light snuffed out so quickly by childhood cancer. After trying for six years to get pregnant, it was almost like some sort of sick and twisted cosmic joke that she would die so young.

Josiah and Kimber seemed to be doing okay. Nobody ever stops mourning or really gets over the death of a child, but so far, about two hours into it, the barbecue was going well, and everyone seemed to be having fun. Kimber and Shannon were friends since first grade, and she felt a bit bad about having not reached out in over three years. Kimber didn't seem angry though, she just seemed happy to have her best friend back again.

About three hours into the barbecue, Kimber approached Shannon and asked her to go into the living room with her to talk. When they got to the room, they were alone, and Kimber gestured for Shannon to sit down at the piano bench. When they were kids, Shannon was always musically inclined and could play almost any instrument effortlessly. Kimber begged Shannon to play something, anything—just for a minute or two. Feeling guilty about the last three years, though thinking it was a really odd request, Shannon obliged and started playing the piano. It was still only her and Kimber in the large living room. All of a sudden about two minutes into the song, Shannon felt something brush up against her ankle. She jumped, startled, and looked over at Kimber. Kimber looked confused and asked her to keep playing. Shannon knew there were no pets or animals in the house but thought she might be a bit tipsy from the alcoholic beverages she had consumed since arriving at the party.

She obliged and again started to play the piano. This time, her wrists were grabbed, and it seemed like little fingers were trying to move Shannon's fingers to other keys. It was as if an invisible force wanted her to play a different tune. That was enough for her. Shannon jumped up off the bench and looked wide eyed at Kimber. "You felt it too, didn't you?" asked Kimber. Shannon was confused and partially terrified and gave her friend a quizzical look. "It's a game Chloe and Josiah used to play. She would crawl underneath the piano, and he would pretend like he didn't know she was there. Then she would come behind him and move his fingers to the right keys because he can't play to save his life, and Chloe was very musically inclined." Kimber was so angry at her friend for setting her up like that she burst into tears, pushed past Kimber, and stormed out of the house. She never looked back and never spoke to Kimber or Josiah again.

65

SILLY PHIL

Hannah and Shasta were neighbors and best friends. They were two independent women of the world and had known each other and been close basically since they were in the womb. Their mothers had also been best friends since childhood, so the women had a kind of sister vibe going on. They were twenty-seven years old, extremely wealthy—independently—and they both loved living next door to each other. They literally shared everything. There was one thing though that they had in common that some might find a bit odd and more than a bit scary. They had a ghost named Phil who would go from house to house and play pranks on each one of them. Phil could technically be considered a sort of poltergeist entity but in a fun way.

Every morning when Hannah would wake up, her cat would be going nuts because Phil had somehow given the animal massive amounts of catnip. He would hide her remote and take her keys. These things were never gone for long though, and when Hannah had had enough of him, she would yell out, "That's it, Phil, it's time to go and visit Shasta." Within seconds Shasta would call her and say, "Thanks! Some friend you are!

Phil is here and has my dogs going nuts!" It was all in good fun, and twenty years later Phil the poltergeist, who plays silly pranks on the girls, still bounces from house to house and messes with the animals and "steals" things.

Nobody knows where he came from or who he was in real life, but the girls seem perfectly happy with Phil being the only man in their lives. When Hannah told me about all of this, I had to wonder if Phil was as silly and playful as he pretended to be. Could it be that he was something that came in through the playful Ouija board sessions the girls had when they first moved into their homes? I wouldn't know because every time I go to visit them, Phil is conspicuously missing. I wonder too if he has some sort of hold on them that they stopped dating as soon as he showed up and if their happiness is sort of like a mirage. Maybe they don't realize he has taken control.

66

THE LADY IN RED AT HUNTINGDON COLLEGE

This one is a legacy at Huntington College in Montgomery, Alabama. It dates all the way back to more than a century ago in 1910, and it's been authenticated by enrollment records and many witness statements from that time and ever since. Legend has it that there is a still unnamed young woman who was enrolled in the college. She didn't have many friends and seemed to be a bit obsessed with the color red. She wore it every day. Red shirts, red pants, red jacket and most of all, she wore a red dress all the time. When asked about this girl before she met her untimely end, witnesses and other kids at the college would describe her as "weird" or "a loner."

Eventually and for some unknown reason, the girl became increasingly isolated. Even on the rare occasion when she was asked out to some social function, she would quickly decline and sit in her dorm room all alone. She became increasingly isolated, and everyone wondered what was going on with her. It seems it all, whatever "it" was, got to be too much for the girl, and she allegedly took her own life by slitting her wrists. When her body was discovered, she was wearing a red gown, which was, by that time, drenched in blood. Ever since the discovery of her bloody body dressed all in red, it's said she haunts the dorms and halls of the university and has been seen by hundreds of people. Both students and faculty today and from years past can attest to sightings of the "lady in red."

67

THE LIGHTHOUSE KEEPER

In 1916 a man named Frederick Jordan was the lighthouse keeper for the Penfield Reef Lighthouse, off the coast of Fairfield, Connecticut. This was one of the most lonely and desolate jobs someone could have. Men would spend weeks or even months alone in these lighthouse towers, making sure everything was working well and that no ships crashed into anything. This particular lighthouse was built in 1874, and this was primarily the way ships were warned of any perils, many of which were so dangerous many a shipwreck could be blamed on them. Their only warning was the lighthouse.

Just before Christmas in 1916, Frederick decided to row home to the mainland to see his family for the holiday. Barely able to even row a few feet, his boat capsized, and he drowned —caught in a gale right outside the lighthouse door.

These days the keepers say the lighthouse is haunted and blame the paranormal activity on Frederick Jordan and his untimely demise. They speak of lighting and equipment malfunctions that seemingly come out of nowhere and that make no logical sense. The scariest reports are those concerning the logbooks. Every once in a while, one of the keepers will report the logbook being open to the exact day in December that Frederick lost his life. It's as if his spirit just wants to make his presence known and be sure he isn't forgotten. So lonely was his life out there alone all of those years ago, way back when, that he wanted to be sure his presence is known and acknowledged now.

68

GHOSTLY CELL PHONE

A few years ago some friends and I were camping in the Pine Barrens in New Jersey. We had gotten a cabin for the weekend and were planning on hunting the Jersey Devil. At the very least we wanted to get some sort of photo or video evidence to prove its presence. We got there early Friday morning and didn't have to leave until late Sunday night.

All in all, the first day was really fun. We had a few drinks, listened to some music, and we were all really enjoying the quiet and solitude this extremely desolate cabin had to offer. There were no other cabins close to ours and no campers either. This was as remote a location as you can get in Central/Southern New Jersey. We even left our cell phones in the car, not that we would have had any service.

Friday night we lit a fire outside and started telling scary stories. We were completely unplugged—no tech—and had agreed to stay that way all weekend. It was about 3 a.m. on Saturday morning when we finally put the fire out and went to bed for the evening. We all admitted we were scared to sleep by ourselves and therefore decided to all sleep in the "living room" area of the small cabin, together, feeling like there would be safety in numbers.

As we were putting our sleeping bags out, though, we all stopped in our tracks as we heard a strange yet somewhat familiar sound. It was as though a voice were talking to us through a cell phone. We all looked around at each other, wondering which one of us broke the rules and brought a cell phone inside the cabin. Each of us said in turn that we swore we hadn't brought our phone in. We were all just standing there, completely still and silent, listening to the sound of a girl screaming for help. The screams and cries were definitely coming from a cell phone. We all searched the cabin, all the while trying to find the source of what we were hearing. The female suddenly started screaming as if in pain and gasping as though she were taking her last breath. It was muffled a bit like it sounds sometimes when you put your phone on speaker and you're going through a bad service area, but we could still hear every single word plain as day. We searched while listening to what sounded like this woman's death cry for at least an hour but to no avail. Finally, after one last extremely loud and dreadfully horrifying scream, the cabin once again went silent. None of us said anything; it was as if we all just knew that was the end of it. We also all knew, though no one said it out loud, that nobody was going to find a cell phone anywhere in, near or around this cabin. What we were hearing was supernatural. It was paranormal and unexplainable. I'm almost positive today that this happened because of my abilities. I hadn't told anyone I was with about being a psychic and physical medium because at the time I was "in the broom closet," so to speak.

We stayed the full weekend but never did go on that hunt for the infamous cryptid. We had had enough with the probable murder we had ear-witnessed our first night there. None of the others ever wanted to speak of it again, so I haven't—until right now.

69

PARANORMAL MUSEUM

In the early 1980s Giles worked in a museum in the western United States. This museum was different from most in that it used to be a prison way back in the early 1900s. Giles used to rent a room in my house, and he would sometimes come home with bruises and burns. It was like every night he was on the losing end of a violent altercation. When I would ask him what was going on, he refused to talk about it and would just go in his room and close the door.

One night he staggered in and fell flat on his face onto the floor right at my feet. I called an ambulance, and we rushed him to the hospital. Giles had a busted lip, a broken nose and two fractured ribs. So what in the world was going on here? Giles was a perfectly normal guy, and we had become fast friends when he rented the room from me. Finally while in the hospital he explained that every night for the past month or so, while he was working the overnight shift at the museum, he had been left alone. The person who was supposed to be working with him on security detail had been cutting out early. Giles said he saw full-bodied apparitions, shadow people and even what he called a demon with glowing red eyes, a grin full of razor-sharp teeth that went literally and unnaturally from ear to ear, and horns at the top of its head. This was a little far-fetched even for me, so I asked if I could go with him to work the next time he went. Obviously he had to heal first.

It took a lot of convincing for him to just not quit, and it seemed those in charge knew quite well what was going on because they didn't question him when he said he needed some time off and explained only that he was injured. They didn't ask how or what happened and didn't really seem concerned in the least. They knew exactly what was going on, and I think they were just happy they weren't being sued or getting in any kind of trouble.

After a couple of weeks, Giles returned to work for his overnight security shift at this museum. I went with him and waited in the car for his partner's inevitable abandonment of not just Giles but of his duties in the gigantic museum. I walked in and was immediately struck by all of the terror and pain lingering in the residuals of this museum. I saw the apparitions Giles had mentioned and even the demon. There were men pleading with me to help cross them over. There were dozens of them, and I promised I would help each one. There was also a woman there whom I came to see was a guest at the prison and who was assaulted and murdered during a riot and breakout back in the 1920s. I crossed over as many men as I could and collected the woman. I took her with me and helped her understand she was dead and needed to move on. It seems she was reliving the terrifying nightmare that was her death over and over again. Night after night she would be violated, beaten and killed again and again. I felt so bad I couldn't even cross her over there.

As far as the shadow entities and demons, I taught Giles how to protect himself. Despite his newfound knowledge, he only worked there for another month or so and never went back. I'm not sure what happened to Giles or where he is today. I only know that about six months after I accompanied him to the museum, he left in the middle of the night and didn't even leave a note. During the final six months he rented the room from me, he became introverted and angry. Lashing out at the smallest things and even at times breaking things like dishes and pictures I had hanging on the walls. I didn't ask him to leave but was insistent he see a priest about an exorcism, as I was sure he had some kind of negative entity, perhaps one or more of those demons, attached to or even possessing him. He raged at the idea and refused every time. I hope Giles is okay. I hope...

70

GRANDMA KIM

In 2012 I was working in a diner again and trying to save enough money to get my own apartment. A friend of mine named Ken, whom I had known from high school, was kind enough to offer me a room in his home a few blocks away from my job. This is the same place where I worked the overnight four-to-four shift and was relieved to have found another place to stay where I could easily get to work. I made sure Ken was aware of my schedule, and he gave me the key to the front door. What I didn't know was that it wasn't just Ken who lived in this house but that it was actually his family home. His father had passed away back when we were in high school, and now it was his sister, his grandmother and his mom. They were all Chinese, and also, Ken was deaf since birth.

I thought that even though I was fluent in sign language, something had gotten lost in translation because every morning when I came through the door to go to my third-floor room, Ken's kindly old grandma would be sitting by the front door in her rocking chair. She would simply stare at me, and I got the feeling she was a bit annoyed by me for some unknown reason. Maybe it was the hours I kept, I don't know. I always said hello and waved, and she always sat stone still except for the rocking back and forth of her chair. His entire family wasn't deaf like him but only spoke Chinese.

My only saving grace here was Ken's fiancée, Alanah. She was only a little bit hard of hearing, and she made me feel very comfortable, and I even started having family meals with them. She also used a fork like me and also didn't speak Chinese. After a few months of living there, I had finally saved up enough money to move into my new apartment. During one of our "family" dinners on my day off, everyone was there. We were all seated at the table for one of Ken's mother's strange-looking yet delicious traditional Chinese meals. All of us except Grandma, that is. She was sitting in her old rocker just watching us with that weird mile-away stare of hers. I thought maybe she was going a bit senile but didn't wanna say that out loud and offend someone after this family had been so good to me.

Towards the end of the meal, after everyone had had a few drinks, I decided to make a toast. I said it in English and signed it too for Ken. I thanked the family for their kindness and hospitality, and I turned to grandma and raised my glass, and in my completely broken and almost completely wrong Chinese, I said, "Thank you, Grandma Kim, for being so lovely as well." This brought gasps from Ken and his mother, and Alanah almost choked on her dessert. When I looked at her and asked what was wrong, she told me that Grandma Kim had passed away six months before I had moved in and that I had been staying in her old room.

71

THE CHAIRS

Rebekah was working at a steakhouse and sports bar, where she rented a room upstairs. She opened for lunch and closed with the bar six nights a week. The bartenders were always the last to leave at around 3 a.m., and it was Rebekah's job to lock the place up after them. She would make sure the side work was done and write down the names of any of the servers or bartenders who hadn't done theirs on any given night. Then she would put all of the chairs on top of the bar and tables and sweep, vacuum and mop the floors.

One night she went into the service area to get herself a drink, and when she went back into the dining room, all of the chairs were already put up. They were stacked neatly on top of the tables, all of them in their proper place and ready for her to start cleaning the floors. The place was rumored to be haunted, but Rebekah didn't believe in such things. That is, until now. She locked the doors and ran upstairs, suddenly now scared to be alone in her own apartment. She had worked there for an entire year, and though she had heard the stories, she herself had never witnessed anything paranormal or even out of the ordinary.

The next day when her boss asked her why she hadn't cleaned the floors and had left all of the chairs and barstools on top of the tables, she hesitantly tried to explain. Her fear now, in the light of day, seemed irrational and even a bit silly. Still she couldn't explain though. Luckily for her, the manager just gave her a knowing smile, handed her the broom, and gave her a quick reminder that they only had an hour before opening for lunch.

72

THE HAT MAN

My friend Steven told me this story, so I am going to write it as he relayed it to me. I was always a strange kid who saw very strange things. I gave up on trying to tell the adults in my life of all the apparitions, black-eyed kids and adults, shadow entities and even demons I was seeing because they always said the same thing or reacted in the same way. They basically assumed I was just, "a strange kid with an even stranger imagination."

When I was nine years old, I went to elementary school in a two-story schoolhouse. The teacher in the classroom next to the one I was assigned to passed me in the hallway, on the stairs, and all of a sudden I was overcome by an icy chill that ran all through my body and up and down my spine. I turned around on the stairs and saw not only the teacher but the black shadow apparition following closely behind him. I was stunned still and silent until my teacher came out of the classroom and broke the spell, asking me if I was okay and if I was planning on attending class that day or just standing at the top of the stairs staring blankly, shocked, into the classroom next door. I apologized but then asked if he, too, had seen the massive, black shadow entity follow the other teacher into the neighboring classroom. He thought it was just a side effect of me walking headfirst into the wall a few minutes earlier while trying to keep my eyes on the apparition and also make my way up the stairs. He wanted me to go and see the school nurse, but I eventually convinced him I was okay, and into the classroom I went. My teacher closed the door behind us.

Over the course of about two months, I would see the huge black shadow following that one teacher around and following behind him wherever he went. Because of my previous success rate with trying to explain to adults what I was seeing, I decided to keep my mouth shut about it. One day as I was in the cafeteria along with a bunch of other students and teachers, the one with the shadow figure following him came in. I could do nothing but stand there and stare, and that was when it happened. The massive blob entity turned, right before my eyes, into a shadow man wearing a hat. It seemed to look directly at me and even tipped its hat to me as I stood, completely dumbfounded, staring at it. I started to shake and cry, and finally one of the lunch aides noticed my terror and asked if I was okay. My dad had to be called to come and pick me up, and needless to say, that was unpleasant.

In the interest of keeping this short, I'll say that within days of my lunchroom encounter, the teacher with the shadow figure in tow stopped showing up to school. After about a month of noticing his absence, I started asking around about what had happened to Mister so and so. I was told, by my own teacher, that Mister so and so had passed away from a heart attack. It seems the day it turned to me and grinned that evil grin—it had taken his life. I often wonder and still wrestle with the guilt of thinking if maybe there was some way I could have warned him. Would it have made a difference? Would he have even believed me anyway? Most likely I would've gotten in trouble for being creepy or telling tall tales, but still, I wish I had been brave enough to have tried to have done or said something. Guess I'll never know.

73

HOSPITAL BEK BOY

'll preface this by stating that the Black-Eyed Kid encounters I've had throughout my life are not the ones you normally hear of. Also, I've been having encounters with them long before they became an internet sensation back in the late '90s. Most of my encounters with them happened when I was in the hospital. I would always be visited by this one little black-eyed boy in particular. He was often by himself but sometimes would be accompanied by other black-eyed kids, boys and girls alike.

The first time I ever saw him, I was twenty-two years old and had been rushed to the hospital due to my body rejecting a simple flu shot. I was stuck in the hospital for almost two weeks, and on the third day of my stay, that was when I first encountered the boy. I was finally allowed to get up and move around, and so I was. I was tired of sitting in the hospital bed and extremely bored. I decided to explore the rest of the floor I was on. After walking around for a little bit, I turned and walked back to my room, and as I did, out of the corner of my eye, I saw a little boy standing by my room's door. I quickly turned away but turned back around almost immediately out of curiosity and the fact that something just seemed off about this kid. He was still standing in front of my door, about ten to twelve feet away from me. He was close enough I could get a good look, and I decided to do just that. He wore blue jean bib overalls and a red and white striped T-shirt. He looked to be between the ages of ten and twelve. I laughed to myself because he resembled Dennis the Menace from the old cartoons I used to watch as a kid.

I watched him for a moment and realized he looked like he was waiting for someone, right there in front of my room. I couldn't see his face at first because his head was down. The nurse walked right past him without even acknowledging him, and to me this was extremely strange because, I mean, what was he doing there. I thought maybe she was thinking he was a guest of mine, but still, shouldn't she at least ask who he was or what he was waiting for? She didn't though, and when she came out of my room a minute or so later, she walked right by him again. It was as if he wasn't even there at all. As she exited my room though, the boy took notice of her and turned to watch her walk past. This was when I finally got a look at his face. His hair was as black as night, which made his pale skin look almost translucent. Just as I started to get extremely uncomfortable and think that maybe I was seeing something I wasn't supposed to, the boy looked me right in the eye and smiled. His eyes were blacker than coal. There was no white to them and no color. Just two black orbs there on his face.

I was startled at the voice behind me of the doctor telling me I had to go back to my room now and that I had had enough excitement for one day. I turned almost too quickly and sputtered out the question of who the little boy was standing there at my room's door. The doctor looked at me quizzically and asked, "What boy?" I turned back around, and the black-eyed boy was nowhere in sight. I was really scared at this point and decided to drop the subject altogether and go back to my room.

Later on when I saw the nurse who had been in and out of my room and whom I had seen pass the boy at least twice, I asked her where he had gone. She smiled at me, a look of concern crossing her face briefly as she put a hand to my head to check my temperature again. Perhaps she thought I was hallucinating from a fever or something. I wasn't warm, and I saw the look of relief cross her face, but she told me she hadn't seen any boy, not in front of my room or anywhere else. The children's floor, reserved for minors under the age of eighteen, was two floors down, and there was no reason for anyone to have been standing in front of my door. She must've sensed how scared I was, and eager to help me feel better, she offered to go and check the guest registry to see who had brought a child in. She figured it was more than likely the boy I saw had been visiting with someone and got bored and wandered off and just happened to have ended up in front of my room. No such luck though as she came back and told me there had been no visitors at all that day, being a slow Sunday, and that I must have overexerted myself walking around like I had and ordered me on bed rest for the rest of the time I was there.

74

BLACK-EYED BOY (PART TWO)

This is a continuation of the previous story. This all took place a few days after I was placed on bed rest by the worried nurse. I was in my room, and it was about eight at night and time for my vitals to be checked before lights out and bed. When the nurse was done checking my vitals, I asked her if she would mind bringing me a snack. She returned a few minutes later with a sandwich and a juice for me, and as she was saying goodnight, it seemed like all hell broke loose in a room down the hall from mine. The alarms started sounding, and someone's booming voice came blaring over the intercom connected to all of the rooms. The nurse told me to stay in bed and went running into the hallway and to the right as fast as she could.

As I looked into the hall, I saw a couple of doctors and a few more nurses all doing the same. I had just been given my meds for the night, including my sleeping pill, so within minutes of the alarm sounding, I was passed out and didn't wake up until morning. I asked the morning nurse what had happened the night before, and she just shrugged and went about her business of taking my temperature and giving me my medications for the day. The nighttime nurse who was there when it all happened got really upset when I asked her and told me it would be against hospital policy if she told me because it concerned another patient. I was annoyed but only because I was so bored I needed the excitement. Looked like I was out of luck.

That is until two days later when I was finally being discharged. For some reason what happened that night wouldn't stop bugging me, and I knew I had to know. I asked the night shift nurse again while I was signing my discharge papers, and she finally relented. Her voice turned to a whisper, and she told me that there was a man a few rooms down from me whose wife was visiting him that night. The man was bedridden, and his wife was sitting in the chair next to his bed, and they were watching some TV. All of a sudden the husband started screaming at the door of his room, though no one seemed to be there, and telling someone or something to go away and to leave him alone. He was screaming, "Leave me in peace! It's not my time yet! I'm not ready yet!" His wife couldn't calm him down and had no idea whom he was screaming at, so she hit the alarm button.

After the nurses assigned to the man went into the room to see what was going on, he began acting out violently. He took his food tray and launched it at the door to his room, all the while ranting and raving about not being ready to die. The nurses couldn't calm him and so hit the alarm to call in the doctors. That was what I had heard that had sent my nurse running after giving me my snack that night. By the time she and the doctors on staff had made it to the room, the man had gone into full-blown cardiac arrest, and his last words were to his wife. He had told her there was a little boy with soulless black eyes who had been harassing him, just standing at the door to his room and smiling at him, for the entire last week he had been there. He died a moment later, and that was that.

The reason my nurse decided to tell me was because she remembered me asking her about a little boy standing at the door to my room and the fact that no one had seen him either.

75

THE DEMON UPSTAIRS

Savannah was twenty-four and finally living on her own. She hadn't moved out of her parents' home after high school because of some medical issues her mother was having at the time. She went to a local community college and commuted from home to school every day. Finally her mother had overcome these issues and was able to live on her own, without assistance again.

Savannah didn't move too far away, only ten short blocks and a phone call away. At least that was what her mother had joked. The apartment complex she moved into though seemed like another planet compared to her mother's large house on the end of the cul-de-sac that she had grown up in. It was in an area of town that was known for homelessness, high crime and violence. Still, she was happy to be on her own finally and living her own life. She was renting a small one bedroom in a completely gutted and newly renovated complex. The building had four small apartments in it. Two upstairs right across from each other and two downstairs. She was the first to move in and was renting the downstairs apartment on the left side. Her first night there was a bit strange. Though she loved the peace and quiet and was sure it wouldn't last very long once the other apartments in the building were rented out, it was a bit creepy being the only one in the entire place at night, all alone.

This all happened in the 1970s, long before cell phones, and at the time, she couldn't even afford a landline on her college allowance and pitiful student's salary. Her mom helped when she could, but medical bills had taken up most of her mother's money, which she inherited from Savannah's father passing away in a tragic construction accident at work when she was just sixteen years old. She tried not to think about it and went about settling in. On her fifth night in her new place, after she had finally finished unpacking everything and when she was just starting to feel settled in, she started hearing strange noises. They were coming from the apartment right above her head. There were sounds like someone was jumping up and down on the floor right above her bedroom and running across the rest of the house too. She noticed after a few days that the activity always started at exactly 3 in the morning. She tried getting in touch with her landlord, but the guy insisted he would see her on the first when he collected her rent, and he told her he would take care of any issues she was having then. She tried speaking to her mom about it, but her mother told her it was just nerves.

Finally one night Savannah, being overtired from being kept up all night again and again, decided to go upstairs and see what was going on. She had convinced herself it was homeless vagrants and that she would just ask them to be a bit quieter and she wouldn't call the landlord or police on them. She made her way up the stairs and knocked on the door, gently at first and then harder and harder until finally all of the noise coming from inside stopped, and the door to the apartment swung open. It seemed immediately that someone or something was inviting her in. Deciding that this was her only chance of getting any peace and quiet, let alone any answers, she pushed her fears to the back of her mind and walked into the place as though she owned it.

As she flicked on all of the lights one by one, she noticed there was absolutely no one in the whole apartment. She was so scared she convinced herself it must be rodents. She knew deep down that there wasn't a known rodent in the world big enough or capable of making the noises she was hearing. It had been like running and jumping, and it had been almost nonstop every time three a.m. would come around. Finally, after calling out to whoever was there multiple times and getting no response, she started to get really freaked out. She turned to run out the front door and back down into her own apartment, but the door slammed shut in front of her and seemed to be supernaturally locked somehow because no matter what she did, she couldn't get it open. That was when she heard a voice calling to her from the bathroom.

The apartment was directly above hers, so it was set up the exact same way. She made her way to the bathroom and once again called out to whoever was there. When she opened the bathroom door, hands shaking so bad she could barely get it open properly, she screamed in horror and terror at what she saw. There in the bathroom was a woman lying in a tub full of bloody red water. A shadow entity stood over her with a shadow knife in its hands. The woman's almost severed arm reached out to Savannah, and the shadow entity turned around, and his sights were suddenly set on her. She ran to the front door, which opened with ease this time, and ran directly out of the building. She drove straight to her mother's house, where, after calming down enough to explain what she had just witnessed, her mother told her about what had happened in the building before they gutted and remodeled the place.

The apartments that used to be there were low-income

housing for students. Five years earlier, all of the apartments were rented to young females, two per apartment, and all of them attended the same school Savannah was attending. One night though, during the winter break, a serial killer had crept through an unlocked window and went from apartment to apartment, murdering every single person in the building. There was only one woman who survived and only long enough to give a statement to the police before slipping into a coma and passing away a month later. She told them everything that had happened and told them she was in the tub when she heard her roommate being murdered, and before she could try to sneak out the window, the man had come for her. The owners of the apartment building decided they wanted to remodel the place and modernize it a bit but still rent to students. There were no disclosure laws back then, and Savannah was stuck staying until at least her lease was up. The killer, by the way, has never been caught.

76

THE WITCH

In 2012 a married couple named Diane and Donnie in Northeastern Pennsylvania bought their first house and moved in with their three kids. It was a huge house with enough room for each kid to have their own room, plus the master bedroom. Before long though, they realized, as most people do, that there was something very wrong, something unnatural about the house they had chosen to spend the rest of their lives in.

Their youngest daughter, Meghan, who was just six years old at the time, started having terrible night terrors and insisted she wasn't having nightmares but that it was all really happening. She described a young girl dressed in old-fashioned clothing coming through her walls at night and approaching her bed. When Meghan would sit up and try to interact with this entity, the girl would suddenly and in an instant grow to be about six feet tall with a haggard face and ratty, dirty gray hair. "The witch" was what young Meghan would refer to the child/old woman as. The old "witch" would grab Meghan by the legs and pull her out of bed, forcing her to her knees and keeping her there with a strong grip on the back of her neck.

With her head being held and being forced to look at the wall just behind her bed, she would see visions that could only be described as hellish. She would tell her parents she was afraid to go to sleep every single night and warn them the "witch" was coming.

Diane decided to sleep in her daughter's room one night to convince the young girl that there was no witch and no little girl, no entities at all or anything that could hurt her in her room. That night Diane lay next to her daughter and waited for her to go to sleep. As she started to doze off herself, she suddenly heard a strange creaking noise, like someone was pacing the floor right next to the side of the bed she was on. This was also the side of the bed the little girl would approach and where Meghan would be pulled onto the floor. Diane looked up and, upon seeing nothing, thought it was just her imagination.

She fell asleep and not long after was woken up by being pulled out of the bed and onto the floor. In a panic she tried to jump up and run but felt she was paralyzed. A haggard and disheveled-looking old woman had a grip on her throat and forced her to look at the wall behind the bed. Diane later described seeing a young woman, about twenty-five years old, dressed in sixteenth-century clothing, standing tied to a stake. She was about to be burned, and Diane somehow knew it was the old witch who now had her in her clutches. She understood the woman was about to be burned at the stake and heard her loudly pronouncing she cursed the land and anyone who dared to try to live on it for the next thousand years. She cursed the souls of the ones burning her and their ancestors too. Suddenly she jumped up and found she was back in her daughter's bed. Diane was shaken up to say the least, but Meghan didn't even seem to have been disturbed and was finally sleeping like a baby through the night.

The next day Diane did some research and saw that back in the mid-seventeenth century, the spot where their house was built was exactly where the town had had their own "witch trials" and saw that there were many curses placed on it. The family moved as quickly as possible and never looked back.

77

EYES IN THE DARK

An eight-year-old boy was visiting his grandfather for the summer, as he did every year, in a small and very poor town in Mexico. It was extremely hot and humid this time of year, and the sun going down didn't offer much relief. There was no air conditioning, and even with the windows open, he still felt as though he couldn't breathe. After lying in his bed for what seemed like hours on end and trying to find a comfortable sleep, he decided to get up and go outside onto the brick patio to get some air.

While out there, he saw his game of jacks and decided to play a few rounds as he tried to wait until he was tired enough that he could sleep without thinking of the heat. The boy played with his jacks until suddenly the ball escaped his grasp and went rolling off the patio and into the yard below. The patio was elevated off the ground kind of like what we call a deck in America. The boy was frustrated because it was pitch black outside aside from the light of the moon, and to an eight-year-old boy, this was a very scary situation. He had no idea how much more terrifying his night would get. He went down the steps to the grass below to see if he could retrieve the tiny ball with a small flashlight his grandfather kept outside for reading.

As he shone the light this way and that onto the grass, something caught his eye. Two huge and inhuman, glowing red eyes were staring back at him from the darkness underneath the patio, just steps from where he was standing. The startled little boy stifled a scream and started to step backwards so he could turn and run, but as he did, he tripped. He was now face to face, eye to eye with these two evil-looking, bright red eyes. He started to slide back on his stomach and suddenly heard a very low and guttural growl coming from where the eyes were. He stood as fast as he could and, on his shaky and petrified legs, ran back into the house and locked the door behind him. As soon as he reached the door, he heard an inhuman and very loud, seemingly angry howl as he took off to his room and hid under his covers for the rest of the night.

As he sat at breakfast the next day, he noticed his grandfather kept looking outside towards the patio with a worried look on his face and was meticulously checking the locks on all the doors and windows even though it was the middle of the day. The boy and his siblings were told they weren't allowed to play outside that day, and when he went to bed that night, his grandfather took up a spot to sleep in a chair, right inside the patio door, with a rifle in his hand.

78

AUNTIE ROSE

J aden and Jessie were twins, and when they were ten years old, they moved into a very old, very creepy-looking farmhouse on the outskirts of Texas. They loved the old house and everything about it. They even loved the kindly old ghost that would visit them from time to time and ask them questions about things they were doing, like homework or playing video games. This seemed perfectly normal to the two kids because even though they knew she was a ghost, she was so friendly and even a bit mothering, they felt they had nothing to fear.

Whenever one of the boys would get hurt, "Auntie Rose" (this was what she asked them to call her, all of their communication telepathic) would suddenly appear with a comforting hug and to wipe the tears away. When they would watch television in the living room, Auntie Rose would sit in a chair in the corner of the room and watch with them. She took a great interest in the boys and almost became like a part of their family.

After about a year of this, and after swearing the children to secrecy about her presence, Aunty Rose started leaving little cups of water on the nightstand for the boys in the middle of the night. They would never wake to drink the water for some reason but always saw the cups in the morning and gave each other a knowing smile.

As the boys got older, their visits with Auntie Rose had gotten less frequent throughout the years, and eventually they stopped seeing her altogether. When they turned eighteen and went off together to college, they were sad to know they would never see the kindly old woman again and wondered what had become of her. At some point in their adulthood they became curious and decided to look up the history of the old farmhouse. They were shocked at what they discovered; a woman named Rose had lived there but had been jailed and eventually hanged for murdering her two nephews. She had left them each a cup of poisoned milk on their nightstand in the middle of the night, and when they woke up thirsty, they had drunk it and died.

79

THE CELL PHONE

Twenty-one-year-old Ricky was sitting in his room one night, charging his phone on his nightstand, when his best friend came through his bedroom door and asked if he wanted to go out to some local bars and get drunk and pick up some girls. Ricky, who didn't have to be asked twice, grabbed his jacket and flew out the door and into his friend's car.

The two hit a bunch of bars that night, and by the time he got home, Ricky was almost blacked-out drunk. He stumbled to his bed and woke up hungover the next morning. Once he got himself together and got into the shower, he realized he didn't have his cell phone with him. He searched his room and even asked his parents if they had seen it. He knew he had grabbed it on his way out the night before, or at least he thought he remembered that, and was in a full-blown panic by the time an hour had passed and there was still no sign of it anywhere. He called the friend he was out with the night before and asked him to check his car but no luck. The friend said he didn't remember much of the night before but was almost certain Ricky didn't have his phone with him the whole night.

Suddenly he remembered he had left it on his nightstand charging when he ran out of the house so quickly the night before. It wasn't there.

Finally he decided to call his phone from his mother's cell phone and was surprised when someone picked up. It was an older-sounding man who said, "Lost your phone, huh, Ricky? There are no cell phones in hell, ya know?" The man then began to laugh maniacally, the sounds of tortured screams throughout the background, and a loud sound, one that sounded like a gigantic, crackling bonfire, came through clear as day as Ricky hung up. He was so shaken up, not to mention confused, he decided to go and lie back down, figuring he would deal with the cell phone issue later on.

When he walked into his room, the first thing he saw was his cell phone. It was right there on the edge of his nightstand, still on the charger. Exactly as he remembered leaving it in such a hurry the night before. There were no missed calls, including any from his mother's cell phone, and he was terrified. He went and got a new phone and a new number the very next day and threw the old phone in the garbage and never thought of it again.

80

THE LADY IN THE BASEMENT

Michelle was babysitting at a neighbor's house one night for an overnight occasion the child's parents were attending. The boy in her care was only five years old, and Michelle was sixteen. She had babysat before, but in all honesty didn't like children very much and just did it in order to make some extra money and to get to hang out in a very large and luxurious home.

Once the boy's parents gave her all of the phone numbers and instructions, they left, and Michelle put the little boy to bed. Though she had never done so before, she decided to disobey the rules and have her boyfriend come over. She figured the five-year-old would be sleeping anyway, and who would it hurt? The little boy seemed to go right to sleep, and within minutes her boyfriend had arrived. He had brought friends with him, three of them, and they were a bit drunk from having had their own party earlier in the night. It was after midnight, and Michelle was starting to rethink ever inviting her boyfriend over in the first place. They were supposed to spend some quiet time together, but his friends were rowdy and loud, and before long, they woke up the little kid.

The boy came out of his room and asked what was going on. Michelle, now in a panic he would tell and she would get into trouble, yelled for him to go back to sleep. This wasn't enough for her boyfriend and his friends though, and they thought it would be funny to make the little boy go and sit on the basement steps—to scare him a little for not staying in his room and sleeping like he was supposed to. The little boy screamed and begged to be let out of the basement for at least three minutes before Michelle had had enough and kicked her boyfriend and his friends out of the house. She locked the door behind them and ran to let the terrified little boy out of the basement.

Once she got to the basement door, however, all she heard was silence, and she decided to listen to hear what was going on. She heard the little boy whispering and thought she heard another very low voice, that of a woman, and even heard the little boy chuckle eventually. Then, much to her surprise, the little boy seemed to have found a way to unlock the door, and he walked out of the basement. He had tear stains on his cheeks, and he gave Michelle a terribly sad look. She went to give the boy a hug and tell him she was so sorry, and also to beg him not to tell his parents, but the boy stopped her in her tracks when he said, "The lady in the basement said you're gonna pay for that!" The basement door swung shut on its own, which should have been impossible, and the boy looked at her and grinned as though he knew something she didn't. He turned and slowly walked up the stairs just as Michelle heard a voice, a woman's, calling out to her from the basement.

81

THE KNOCKING

When Evan was ten, he was suddenly afraid to go to sleep at night. He had been in the same room since he was born and hadn't ever had any issues before, until his tenth birthday. That very night, after celebrating with his family at home, something seemed different about his room when he lay down to go to sleep, but he couldn't quite put his finger on what it was. He was woken up in the middle of the night by a strange knocking sound that at first seemed to be coming from outside his window. That wasn't possible though; even at ten Evan knew that nothing and nobody could knock on a second-floor window. There were no large trees outside, so it couldn't have been branches.

After about a week of his being woken up to this knocking, Evan finally got up enough courage to go to the window and see what it was that was making the noise. It was probably as his father had said and something completely benign and explainable. There was nothing there though, and as he listened and heard the knocking again, as he stood at the window looking out into the yard, he realized now it was coming from the wall on the far right of the room. He jumped back in bed, hid under the covers, and finally fell back asleep. It went on like this for another week or so, with the knocking seeming to come from one place and, when investigated, actually coming from somewhere else altogether. Evan eventually learned to ignore it because there was never anything other than some benign knocking.

One morning though, after about two months of the ever-relocating knocking in his room, Evan got up and started getting ready for school. He looked in his bedroom mirror and fixed his hair. He wanted to make sure he didn't have anything in his teeth, and he leaned into the mirror and smiled. He immediately jumped back as he recognized the image in the mirror was not at all of his face or his teeth but of jagged and bloodstained fangs. When he leapt back and looked again, he saw a grotesque version of himself. Smiling with those horrible teeth from literally ear to ear was a face with skin peeling off and landing in chunks on the table next to him. He screamed and ran out of the room. That night when he went to bed, he thought about covering up the mirror but was too exhausted from the terror of thinking about what had happened that morning all day and just went to bed. He was once again woken up by the strange knocking, only this time it was coming from inside the mirror.

82

THE KITTEN

I will never forget this for as long as I live, and it happened so long ago. Ever since it happened, my mother refuses to even acknowledge it occurred let alone give me any sort of explanation for it. When I was four years old, I heard a strange sound coming from the basement of our house. It sounded just like a little baby kitten. Being a toddler, I was curious and wanted to see the kitty and bring it into the main house to keep as a pet. Even at that age I knew it was weird to keep a kitten trapped in a basement when there was a perfectly fine and loving home for it right there at the top of the stairs.

At dinner was when I would hear it the most, with the basement door and steps being right there in the kitchen across from the dinner table, but every time I would ask about the kitty in the basement, my father would look worriedly at my mother, and she would tell me to be quiet and finish my meal. I would shrug and finish eating and look longingly at the basement door as I walked past to go upstairs and back to my room to play. I was an only child, after all, and quite lonely. I didn't make friends easily, and back then there weren't such things as playdates. Four-year-olds didn't get out much outside of the family unit and home.

Finally, after about a year of hearing this kitten make noises in the basement, they sounded so sad to me, I decided I was gonna go down into the basement and play with it. My young mind knew I would get into trouble but also was starting to feel really bad for this poor little animal I was sure was being purposefully trapped down there by my parents for whatever reason. I mustered all the courage I had, and when my parents were in the living room watching TV one night, I made my move. I opened the basement door and went down the steps towards the sound of the little kitten. Suddenly it was more like the roar of a giant wild cat, and before I could react, I was yanked backwards and back up the stairs by my mother. Instead of scolding me though, she offered me some cake. She even said I could eat it in my room as long as I promised not to come out until she or my father came and got me.

I'm not sure how long I was made to sit in my room that night, but eventually, long after I went to bed, I heard my parents come in to tuck me in. They pulled up my blankets over me and kissed my head, turning off the light as they left my room. I never heard the kitten or any other noise for that matter coming from the basement again. I always wondered why that little boy was making kitten noises in the basement, and why he had no arms or legs.

83

SPIRIT FAMILY

One night while staying at my dad's apartment after my parents divorced, I jumped up suddenly to see two strange-looking figures standing at the foot of my bed. I would say they were staring at me, but I couldn't tell because they were just shadows. I felt like I was being watched and was just about to scream when suddenly it felt like something was covering my mouth. I then heard a male voice say, "Where is she?" Then I felt whatever it was lift from my mouth, and all I could mutter was a faint response with my voice quivering. I said, "I don't know," and shrugged. Somehow I wasn't scared anymore, but the shock and weirdness of it all had me thinking maybe this was some sort of lucid dream. Plus, I knew a little bit about the paranormal due to my mom being a "witch" and growing up around that sort of thing my entire life. The "male" figure and the "child" whose hand he was holding turned and walked through the wall on the left side of the room.

Within minutes another, lone shadow person came through the right side of the wall in my room and stood at the bottom of my bed; again I felt like it was staring right at me. I jumped up, and it spoke in a loud female voice, telepathically this time, "Where are they?" I just assumed she was asking about the "man and child" who had been there minutes before, and I silently pointed to the left wall. "She" quickly turned and walked through the left wall.

I'm not sure what was going on or why I saw these spirits as shadows when I had seen ghosts a dozen times before and they always appeared to me normally, or as normally as a spirit or ghost can appear to a human. I never had any more problems in that little apartment and was never really scared of what I had seen and heard, aside from in those first few moments. I like to think they were a family who somehow lost each other and found each other again on the other side thanks to whatever was happening in my room, which allowed them to come through on that night so long ago.

84

INHUMAN SCREAMS

A family of four were all asleep one night in their respective bedrooms when they all suddenly started hearing loud, bloodcurdling screams coming from somewhere inside the house. With a mother and two teenage daughters, they each thought it was one of the others, and they all came running out into the hallway where all of the bedrooms led to. The man of the house, the father, saw that all three women were accounted for and sent them all into the master bedroom while he went and checked the rest of the house. He walked through each and every room, all the while still hearing the screaming, which had now turned to intermittent growling, but could find nothing.

Once he made two rounds about the house, the screaming/growling stopped, and they all went back to bed. Though they were scared, they were a very religious family who didn't believe in such things as ghosts or spirits and didn't really know how to explain it or what to do about it except to move on and try to forget the whole thing. This went on though, every single night for an entire week before finally they decided to gather, in the middle of the night while the screaming and growling was going on, and read out loud together from their Bibles. This seemed to have some kind of effect at least as the growling became much more prominent, and the screaming stopped altogether. The terrified family kept reading verse after verse all as one and together until finally the front door flew off of its hinges, and a giant breeze blew through the house, almost knocking the four people over, seemingly on its way out the door.

85

THE LADY WITH LONG BLACK HAIR

Marcy was staying with her mom during the divorce with her two young sons aged four and seven. The boys had their own room there and played in it for hours on end. This was concerning for Marcy because it seemed her kids were becoming withdrawn; they had never played for so long together without needing her for something or fighting. She was beginning to wonder how badly the divorce was really affecting them. Every time she went into their room to check on them though, they were laughing and giggling and playing, so she figured they couldn't be doing too bad.

One day she went in to tell them it was time for lunch, and she asked the boys what they were giggling about. They told her "the lady with the black hair is funny." Marcy played along and didn't discourage them from having an imaginary friend. It didn't seem to occur to her, as a nonbeliever in the paranormal, why her two young sons would make up a friend who was a grown woman.

After a few weeks though, she decided she wanted to take the boys on a picnic and get them out of the house for a while. They spent all of their time now playing in their room with each

247

other and "the lady with the long black hair." When she walked in, she saw her youngest son sitting on the floor and looking up at his brother, who had her brush in his hands and was pantomiming brushing someone's long hair. She was suddenly very creeped out and asked what they were doing. They responded by saying they were brushing the lady's hair. She hurried them out of the room, and they went on with the rest of their day and had a lovely picnic. When they got back home, she got the boys ready for bed and tucked them in, for once not thinking about the creepy incidents occurring more and more around the home, which the boys were blaming on this "lady with long black hair."

The next morning Marcy searched for her brush and then remembered her sons had been using it to play with their imaginary friend. She snuck into their room to grab it and saw, to her horror, it was filled with long, black hair. Marcy was the only one in the house with long hair at all, and hers was blonde.

86

THE LAMP

While on vacation with my boyfriend a few months ago, something happened that still scares the living daylights out of me and that I just cannot explain for the life of me. We stayed at a five-star hotel and had an amazingly romantic time.

My issue comes with something that was happening at night. Every single night we were there, I was startled awake at 3:30 in the morning hearing a noise coming from the foot of the bed but further along the wall and to the right. There was a long shadow entity there, and it was a bit of a weird shape. It always seemed somehow like I was catching this thing by surprise, whatever it was, and it would stand completely still the minute my eyes were on it. I would be convinced in the middle of the night that this was an entity even though when I woke up in the morning, I could plainly see a lamp was there. A large, standing black lamp was in the exact same spot. This was obviously my mind playing tricks on me, but no matter how many times I saw this lamp during the day, when I would wake up in the middle of the night and see it there, I somehow just KNEW it was a shadow entity of some sort. I can't explain it and just tried to put it out of my head except I just got home and looked through all of the pictures, paying particular attention to the ones taken in the room. There is no lamp in any of the more than a hundred photos we took in and of that hotel room. My husband thinks I'm losing my mind, as he is certain there never was a lamp there.

87

CURSE OF VENGEANCE

A nother true haunting that took place in the early 2000s involved a demonic entity. A man named Bob Cranmer and his entire family lived with and were incessantly tormented, in unimaginable ways, by an actual demon. After various forms of assaults, injuries and even the deaths of some of their pets throughout the years, in 2005 the family finally decided to have a priest come and perform an exorcism in the Godforsaken home. The family claimed that the walls would bleed, and they lived in constant fear for their lives. The church agreed to allow the exorcism, and some interesting information about why this house contained the demonic entities it did and their purpose for being there was uncovered.

It seems the man who built the house placed a curse on it because a group of Native Americans allegedly slaughtered a bunch of settlers who were inhabiting the land way back in the 1800s, and he wanted to make sure, or so it seemed, any of the Natives who thought they were going to take over the land of the people they slaughtered were never going to rest there in peace—while alive or after death. Another claim as to why the demon or demons were attracted to this particular house is that there was a doctor there who performed illegal procedures and unmentionable experiments on unwilling patients who had somehow attracted the evil.

While it's unknown if Bob believes in the Native American curse, he has made it clear he believes that the doctor did in fact attract the evil to the home with his wicked deeds done in the dark of the house's basement. He claims the man was a devil worshiper and even went so far as to allege the doctor sacrificed children. It's often alleged that, even after the exorcism, the family had undergone so many years of torment and terror, every single one of them had to spend some time in a psychiatric hospital in order to get help in recovering from the ordeal.

88

THE CRYING LADY

Visiting my mom's house is always an adventure. Being a physical medium makes her haunted house quite the experience even when I am just there for a simple weekend visit.

When you walk through her front door, there is a living room area and then a den, a kitchen and dining room, and then upstairs there is a bathroom and three bedrooms. The room on the right belongs to my seventeen-year-old son, Damien, who is also a physical medium. The room to the left of his is my mother's room, and then my room is to the left of hers.

After a long morning of running errands and grocery shopping, all three of us retired to our respective rooms to rest and take a nap. Within ten minutes I heard what I thought was my mother crying. My stepfather, whom she was married to for thirty-two years, had just passed away this past February, so I thought maybe my mom was upset about that, and it took me a minute or two to decide if I should go and offer her some comfort. With my mom being so put together and unemotional as she is a lot of the time, at least publicly, I wasn't sure if it would just upset her more that I had heard her. I decided to go and knock on her door and see if there was anything I could do.

As I came out of my bedroom, my son also came out of his at the exact same time, and we both just looked at each other. He said to me, "Oh, I was just about to knock on your door and make sure you were okay. I heard crying coming from your room." I explained it wasn't me and that it must be Mom (which is also what he calls my mother). We shrugged it off, and I went to knock on my mother's door even though none of us could hear the crying anymore. Just as I raised my hand to knock, my mother opened her door, and a look of concern was on her face. Her eyes were dry, and she jumped and asked what the hell we were doing standing around by her door like that. We explained to her that we had heard crying and assumed it was her since Damien, originally thinking it was me, saw that it wasn't. She looked extremely confused and then a bit scared as she explained she was just coming out of her room to knock on my door so we could make sure Damien was okay, as she had heard crying coming from his room. We all stood there for a moment, puzzled and a bit frightened, but decided to just let it go and go back to our own rooms.

As soon as we all turned to go back into our respective rooms, all three of us heard the distinct sound of someone crying coming from the bathroom, which was also right there, just steps in front of us in the tiny upstairs hallway. The door was wide open, and we could all plainly see there was no one in there, crying or otherwise. Also, there was no other living person in the house other than the three of us. We all quickly turned and went back into our rooms and never spoke of it again. The crying lady is one of the many ghostly sounds I hear when staying at my mom's house, and she is definitely the one I hear most often.

89

THE WHISPERING PICTURE

This story is very similar to one I have already written previously in this book, but because these are true encounters, some things are bound to have happened more than once. Cindy and her cousin Angelica were having a sleepover one night at Angelica's house. She lived there with her mother, Shirley, and her father, Merle. The girls were teenagers and were doing things teenage girls do, like talking about whom they had a crush on and painting each other's nails. This was back in the '90s before the internet, and you actually had to keep yourself occupied with your imagination in order to have a good time.

They were supposed to be in bed with lights out by midnight, but after Cindy's aunt had come in and shut the lights off and said her goodnights, the girls suddenly started hearing whispering in the dark. The room was pitch black, as it was considered uncool to have a night-light, and each of the girls was wondering if the other one heard it.

After about five minutes of silence, aside from the very low and feminine-sounding whispering, Cindy finally asked Angelica if she was hearing anything strange. Angelica immediately sat up and turned the lamp on next to the bunk beds. She was almost in tears as she related to Cindy that she was hearing whispering, and it sounded like it was her long-deceased grandmother's voice. Angelica had been very close to her grandmother before she died of cancer when she was ten years old. It was her father's mother, and since she and Cindy were related on the maternal side, this was not Cindy's grandmother too.

After discussing for a moment the probability that Angelica's dead grandmother could be actually whispering something unintelligible to them there in the darkened room in the middle of the night, they decided to keep very still and quiet and see if they heard it again. As soon as they stopped to listen, they heard what could only be considered a low growl, and they both looked above the bed to the picture of Angelica's deceased grandmother. The picture had a snarl on her grandmother's face instead of the kind smile, and as they sat there and watched in horror, her eyes moved from one to the other, and the mouth yelled, "OUTSIDE!" The girls screamed at the top of their lungs and ran for their lives into the hallway.

Angelica's mother came running out of her room, asking what in the world was going on and why the girls were screaming like that. Shirley immediately saw both teenagers shaking and crying hysterically, so upset they couldn't explain at first what was happening. Finally Shirley calmed them down enough, downstairs over a cup of tea, that they were able to recount what had just happened in the room.

Before they could get very far though, the family's car alarm went off outside, and when they looked out the window, there was a strange man who looked like he had just been near the car and was now walking towards the garage. Sure enough, the garage door handle started jiggling, and thank goodness it was locked. By the time the police arrived, the man had long since given up and left the premises, but all three females were pretty sure had the girls not received that terrifying visit from Angelica's deceased grandmother, they would not have caught the man trying to break in, and who knows if he would have come back and perhaps gotten into the house.

Though it was a scary visit, it ended up helping them in the long run, and given the kindness of old grandma Agnes, they all knew she scared them so the situation would play out exactly as it did and the man could be caught in time. Still, there is no longer a picture of Grandma Agnes above Angelica's bed. It's just too creepy now.

90

AMITYVILLE

Every book that contains true and real-life, terrifying ghost stories needs at least one great and well-known legend of the times. I chose Amityville for this one, and I'm sure, if you're reading this title, you will know what that one word means. Ron DeFeo, Jr. murdered his entire family one night, seemingly out of the clear blue sky, and then went to the local bar and had a drink or went to work at his grandfather's car dealership, depending on who's telling the story. There are so many accounts and legends surrounding this particular case that it's hard to know what's what and what's real. I think I found at least a little bit of the truth and felt I had to share it here.

Amityville is a village in Suffolk County on Long Island in New York State. Amity was considered back in the 1970s and, still is today, an upscale community and safe place to live. This little village was made famous because of something that happened there on November 13, 1974, at 112 Ocean Avenue. At around six in the morning, a resident who was out taking his dog for a walk noticed something unusual about his neighbor's house. These neighbors were the DeFeos, and they were made up of mother Louise (forty-two), father Ronald, Sr. or "Big Ronnie" (forty-three) and their five children. The children were Ronald or "Butch," who was twenty-three at the time, Dawn (eighteen), Allison (thirteen), Marc (twelve), and John Matthew (nine). What the neighbor noticed was that all of the lights on the third floor were on, and he had never seen that before. He would have noticed it because his routine was taking his dog past their house at the same time every morning.

At 6:30 that morning, the oldest of the DeFeo children, "Butch," was found behind the wheel of his car at work at his grandfather's car dealership. That morning another neighbor of the DeFeos showed up to take the younger children to school, but, though both cars were in the driveway, nobody answered the door. This woman dropped her children off and then went back to try again at around 8 a.m. This neighbor's name was Catherine, and she went back to the DeFeos' for a third time at 5 p.m. and got no response again, despite both cars still being there. The elder Ron DeFeo also didn't show up for work, and young Marc never showed for his physical therapy appointment either. Even the mailman noticed the family's dog didn't incessantly bark at him when he arrived at ten a.m. and knew that the dog was only quiet when it was tied up in the backyard—he saw it wasn't. It seemed the only one of the DeFeos who could be accounted for was Ronald Jr./Butch.

At 6:30 p.m. after putting in a full day's work doing odd jobs at his maternal grandfather's car lot, Butch DeFeo ran into a local bar visibly upset and screaming, "You have to help me! Someone shot my mother and father!" Butch and a bunch of other bar patrons piled into their cars and raced to the DeFeo home. Butch refused to go into the home and insisted on staying outside in the car. The other men went in, and in the master bedroom they saw Louise and Big Ronnie lying on their stomachs with blood all over them. A man named Joel ran downstairs and called 911.

Another man named John A. went to check the children's rooms and found a very bloody, eerie and grisly sight, as all four of the DeFeo children who were in the home were also deceased. Officer Kenneth Greguski arrived on the scene and confirmed the entire family had been murdered. No one had any news of his sisters yet, so Butch told the police they also were in the home when he left that morning, and it was then confirmed that they, too, had been murdered. To keep this a condensed version of the story, let's get to Ronald DeFeo, Jr.'s confession.

91

AMITYVILLE 2

After blaming the murder on multiple other people and giving countless theories to the police, DeFeo finally confessed. There were so many strange things about the case that just weren't adding up for the police. There were no drugs found in any of the victims' systems, yet none of them had moved from their beds, which meant they hadn't heard the others being murdered or even the gunshots. Surely there was one who was killed first, and the others heard it and so on, but there was no evidence anyone ever left their beds or even woke up except Big Ronnie.

It was a known fact that Big Ronnie had an explosive temper and abused every single one of his children and his wife. The abuse on Ronnie, Jr. started when he was only eighteen months old. Young Ronnie would inherit his father's violent and explosive temper, and by the age of seventeen was hooked on drugs. By the time he murdered his family, he was drinking a fifth of scotch and shooting multiple bags of heroin daily.

Ronnie Jr.'s defense claimed he heard voices and even that he was possessed by the devil during the shootings. It's alleged that Jr. himself said that upon waking up the morning of the murders, he had been sitting in the basement after being kept up all night hearing voices telling him to kill his family and then himself. He even claimed a shadow entity in the shape of a man appeared out of the wall and handed him the gun, saying, "Do it!" He then was in a trance and possibly possessed as he went up the stairs and murdered each member of his family in cold blood, one by one.

The paranormal element doesn't stop there, as people often wonder how nobody seemed to have heard anyone else being murdered. Was this some sort of paranormal or supernatural element to the case? Had Jr. accepted the rifle from the devil himself, and then some sort of spell was cast over the house? The neighbors never heard any shots either. It would make sense that, when two people are asleep in close proximity to each other—like in the same room—when the first one is attacked or shot, the other would wake up and try to flee and run for their lives. This didn't seem to happen though, and many people believe it is very likely that some sort of demon was in the home, possibly multiple, due to the extreme violence being carried out there on a regular basis. We will never know, as Ronald DeFeo, Jr. passed away in March in 2021. He had changed his story so many times, but for the most part and especially during the trial, he claimed and was adamant he was taken over by some sort of evil that made him do what he had done that awful morning.

This is not the first case of guilt by demonic possession in which there are eerie facts that make no sense except to be supernatural, and it certainly wasn't the last. There is so much rumor built up around this case we will never know the real answers. Five people lost their lives, and the next family to buy the home was allegedly terrorized by the supernatural to the point where they had to leave the home with all of their possessions in it and run. Is this house a gateway to hell? Is it the home of the devil and his minions? Do they sit and lie in wait for some angry soul to move in or cross paths with the property so it can feed and take over their minds, eventually possessing them to kill? Be careful of the negative energy you allow yourself to carry, or one day we may be asking these questions about your home. If it can happen in a small and seemingly safe village like Amityville—it can happen anywhere.

92

EVIL LURKS

In my mid-twenties all I did was work during the day and karaoke at night. It was a good life for me, and all I really did was have fun. I drank a lot when I would go to karaoke though, and because I was, at the time, a diner waitress, keeping a roof over my head was hard. I would be too hungover to go in for the early mornings and long hours on my feet. Luckily I drove, and I live in New Jersey, which has the most diners in it in the entire country.

After losing another job due to my late night activities and therefore not being able to pay my rent, I once again was forced to move. I had a friend who was a bit older than me whom I had met at my last job, though, named Darla, and she had kind of taken me under her wing. Despite my no longer working with her, I guess she felt bad for me and offered me the basement apartment of the home she owned with her husband. In exchange I would help watch their kids every so often and help her when she needed it with running errands and things like that. It was a great offer, and the apartment, though small, was really pretty amazing. It was perfect for me, and she didn't care if my boyfriend stayed or really what we did. We agreed once I got a job, I would pay a small amount for rent and still continue helping her as needed with whatever she asked.

She had lived in the house for ten years and said she had never rented the basement out, and she also never used it, so it was brand new. I should have known it was too good to be true, but I suppose I wasn't worldly enough yet at that time, and also I was desperate. I moved in right away and without incident. Immediately upon entering the basement though, I knew something was wrong; though I had long ago turned my abilities off, for lack of a better way of saying that, I still knew when evil was around. I didn't want to complain though, and at that time in my life I kept the fact that I had any abilities at all quiet for fear of judgment. I ignored the creeping feeling as best I could even though it got worse day by day. After a series of small but concerning things that I had allowed my skeptical and downright non-believing boyfriend to talk me and himself out of, it got to the point I could no longer ignore it.

One night after coming home late from karaoke, I took a shower before bed. I was drunk, and my boyfriend couldn't stay that night. I was all by myself in the apartment. When I got out of the shower, I felt better. That is until I looked up and saw on the mirror, written in the steam from my very hot shower, "You'll Die Here." I wiped it as fast as possible and went to bed, the entire time knowing there was a malevolent presence there with me. Luckily, I had consumed enough alcohol that I was able to pass out despite being watched all night and knowing it.

A couple of nights later, again I had an incident in the bathroom. This time my boyfriend was staying over, and I was in there showering, and he was in my bed, watching TV. The bathroom led right into the bedroom. I was washing my face and heard the shower curtain open up. I said something playful to my boyfriend about joining me, and a very low, very menacing voice said, "Well, if that's an invitation," and I suddenly felt a freezing cold claw like hand on my shoulder. I spun around and ran out of the bathroom without even putting a towel on. I was about to start screaming to my boyfriend what had happened, but he was already standing by the door, staring wide eyed at it without moving. It was like he was in a trance or something. I screamed, and he just said, "I saw it walk in there!" The both of us cuddled in bed that night and neither got much sleep. He and I broke up not too long after, as I never wanted to stay at his place because of his five gross roommates, and he didn't want to come to mine after the bathroom incident.

I lived there for about another month but couldn't take any more after that. The final straw was a very intimate attack while I was sleeping. When I went to explain to Darla, the woman who had given me the place to stay, why I couldn't stay there anymore—that's when the scariest thing happened. She said, "Ohhh, what's the matter, little Gemma? Can't face our own demons, can we?" I turned and ran as she laughed maniacally behind me. She yelled after me, "You can't escape us, you know!" I didn't even turn around and had some other friends go and move me. I know it's possible for a person to literally bring to life their own personal demons, but that wasn't what was going on because it stopped right after I left that place. I'm not sure what was going on, but I never heard from Darla again, and I definitely don't even pass that house anymore while going anywhere. I live close by it now and am terrified I will somehow pick whatever that was back up and bring it home with me—especially with how open I have become with my abilities.

93

STRANGE POSSESSION

A friend of mine named Terry told me this story, and I knew I had to put it in this book. She told me about how in the late eighties she worked in a convenience store in one of the Bible Belt states here in America. Being from New Jersey originally, it was like a whole new world. I asked her about her scary experiences because, with a lot of the same gifts I have, I knew she would have a ton of them.

She explained to me that one night while she worked the overnight shift in one of these little gas station convenience stores, a man came in who looked like there was something off about him. Mind you, he didn't really "look" like this, not to anyone but Terry or someone like her anyway, she was looking with her psychic eyes, so to speak. On him she saw blood and death, murder and absolute evil.

As the man approached her to pay for his gas, she backed away a bit and was wondering if she should mention to him that his soul was in real danger. She decided to keep it to herself and just try to be as normal and calm as possible with so much evil literally almost coming out of this guy's pores. He must've seen her back up because he gave her a huge, toothy grin and tipped his hat to her. "How are you doin', ma'am?" he asked her in what she knew to be a very fake Southern drawl. She responded with, "I'm okay, thank you. That'll be ten dollars even for the gas." The man hesitated a moment and gave her an odd look. He reached into his back pocket, and suddenly Terry could see the demons leeched on to the man, and they all dispersed from his body for just a moment, looked her in the eyes, and hissed at her. The man looked confused, and I'm sure Terry looked horrified and shocked herself. The man put the money on the counter, but before he left, he turned to her and said, "Lady, it seems to me it's your lucky night. Don't waste your gifts." Just like that he exited the store, got in his vehicle and left. Terry was able to shake this off and move on rather quickly; such is the life of people like us, I suppose.

The next morning when she woke up, she sat with her coffee in front of her television and was shocked at what she saw. Nine gas station convenience stores had been robbed the night before, and in every single one of them the cashier and gas attendant were killed. Knifed to death, and in some cases some of the money was even left behind. It was like a madman was simply out for blood. They never arrested the guy, or if they did, she never found out because she left that place within a month or so and never looked back. What she saw that night was a possessed man. The entities possessing him, however, knew Terry's power and the power in her gifts. They also knew who those gifts came from, and somehow they either decided not to or weren't allowed to act in violence against her.

94

SNOWED IN

Melissa was seventeen years old when she and her parents went to a cabin in upstate New York and rented it for the week, with the full intention of getting snowed in. It was something they did every year, and I never understood it. That same year she invited me, and even though I thought it was weird, I wanted to go because she was my best friend, and I knew regardless of the weather, it would be a lot of fun.

Melissa's parents were young and were always playing jokes on one another, and really the whole family played pranks on one another all the time. It was always a happy time when I was with them, and I laugh often when remembering the sleep-overs I had over at her house. By this age though, Melissa would just become embarrassed by her parents, her dad in particular, whenever he would try to play a prank on her or her friends. While I found it charming, she would scream and yell. It didn't stop her dad though, as, like almost all parents, he thought embarrassing her was cute or something since she thought she was too grown to laugh.

We got to the cabin around one in the morning, and we

were all pretty much too tired to do anything but sleep. The next day we had a full day of having snowball fights, building snowmen and even making snow angels. It was turning out to be a really great vacation even as someone who under normal circumstances couldn't stand the snow and would much prefer to be indoors when it fell or was even on the ground. My favorite part of this really amazing cabin was the multiple fireplaces. One of them was in the room Melissa and I were sharing, and her dad was nice enough to let us have a fire going while we hung out. This was the late '90s and right before the internet age hit, so we did what normal teens back then did and stayed up just talking for hours on end and well into the middle of the night. There were no phones in the cabin either, and even if everyone did have a cell phone back then, which they definitely didn't, it wouldn't have worked in these far out of the way cabins in the mountains anyway.

It was around 3 a.m. when the fire finally went out, and she and I were tired enough to go to sleep. She reminded me her dad would most likely come into the room at some point just to make sure the fire was out and not to be scared. I told her okay, and we went to bed. Within fifteen minutes of turning all of the lights off, my best friend was already sleeping, and I knew this because she snored.

Just as I started to drift off a couple of minutes later, a figure appeared at the door and stuck its head in, and because I was almost completely asleep, it startled me at first. I knew it wasn't a ghost or anything because I experienced those all the time with my "gifts." I also knew it was specifically Melissa's dad because he was wearing his Yankees World Series Champions shirt he had been wearing when we said goodnight to him earlier. I expected him to come into the room and just check the fire, but he just stood there, seemingly dazed and staring at the bunk beds we were sleeping in, probably thinking we were both asleep. I closed my eyes as much as I could while still making sure I was able to see at least a tiny bit because I was starting to feel weird about this situation.

Needless to say, the situation did get really weird and fast too. Before I knew it, her dad was standing next to our beds, and I was on the bottom, so his face was right next to Melissa's. He smelled like death and formaldehyde, and it was all I could do to keep from gagging. As I raised my hand to my mouth to stop from coughing or making any noise, all of a sudden his face was directly in my face, and I just lost it. I screamed at the top of my lungs, knocked her dad over, and went running out of the room to go and get her mother. I heard Melissa running after me, but I wouldn't stop. I burst into her parents' room and was going to ask her mom what the hell was wrong with her husband scaring us like that, but then I was the one who must have looked crazy. Melissa's mother jumped out of bed and switched the light on the second I slammed the door open yelling like I was. Only, her father also jumped up in the bed, looking confused. I was screaming and crying incoherently and wouldn't let her father comfort me and insisted her mother come down to check out the room.

She did, with Melissa's father following close behind, not wanting to get too close 'cause I would scream and shake every time he did. When we got into our room and turned the lights on, nobody was there. They finally calmed me down, and by this time the sun was coming up. I told them all what had happened, and her father got angry thinking this was all some kind of elaborate prank Melissa and I had planned to get him back for something he had done earlier in the day. Finally they sent us back to bed and refused to listen anymore. They were angry. I stayed up all night, and though I insisted I wanted to go home as soon as they all finally woke up the next day, they weren't bringing me and couldn't, as we were snowed in now from all the snowfall that came overnight.

By week's end the whole family believed me and weren't angry anymore, but they never mentioned it again, and it kind of messed my relationship with Melissa up because even though it wasn't her father, and I know now what it really was, I couldn't ever look at him without thinking of the terror of that night.

95

IT

Gianni would often visit his grandparents in Italy, and up until he was a teenager he always looked forward to those visits. It wasn't until he turned fifteen that he had this intense foreboding of going to visit their home. He couldn't explain it and surely couldn't say it out loud, but there was something inside him telling him not to go this time. He would be there for a few weeks in the summer and knew it would break his grandparents' heart, so he went anyway and tried to suppress the odd feelings he was having about it.

Once he got to Italy, it was the same as always, and there was a huge party with tons of home-cooked Italian food to welcome him. He had many relatives other than his grandparents who lived there, and before long those feelings of dread had passed.

After a long night of celebration and eating, and a lot of drinking by the adults, it was time for bed. Gianni went upstairs to the loft where he slept and closed his eyes to go to sleep. He couldn't sleep though, not tonight. He had never had trouble before and especially not on his first night there with so much activity to tire him out. He wanted to just go for a walk though he knew he would be in big trouble if he did. His grandparents were extremely superstitious and believed that shapeshifters, demons and goblins roamed around the small village at night, looking for humans to possess and take over so they could live again or live at all in the case of the nonhuman entities. He thought all of this was nonsense but had always respected their wishes—until now. He just couldn't stop tossing and turning and decided to sneak out and go for that walk anyway. His grandparents never even locked their doors and slept all the way across the house from him, and therefore getting out and back in wouldn't be hard at all.

It was around one in the morning when he exited his grandparents' home and walked onto the street. He started his walk around the block, but it was pitch black. There were no streetlights at this time in this village, and he kept psyching himself out with every little noise he heard. Was that cat meowing really a shapeshifter or lost soul? Was that rat that crossed his path a shapeshifting demon? He laughed to himself, but he wasn't laughing for long. All of a sudden as he rounded the bend to turn the corner that should've been his grandparents' street, he realized somehow he had taken a wrong turn. He knew this wasn't possible because he had only made three right turns so far, and one more right turn should have him back at their house. He immediately panicked once he looked around and realized he was all the way on the other side of the village. There was so much fog, and combined with the darkness, he couldn't see two feet in front of him. He only knew where he was because he was in front of the one gigantic church in the whole place.

Regardless of how he had gotten there, he knew he needed to make it back to his grandparents' house and soon. He started to walk as fast as he could without really being able to see. Suddenly he heard loud footsteps behind him. Not only that, he could feel the breath of someone, or something, behind him as well. Tears started to fall from his eyes, and he couldn't breathe. He walked faster and faster and was terrified to turn around. He knew he wasn't just tricking himself, something was there, and it was almost right on his back.

As he walked faster and faster and cried harder and harder, he suddenly heard a voice coming from behind him, saying, "Slow down, Gianni, just for a moment. A moment is all I will need." It was an evil and wicked voice, and what followed it was a deranged and sickeningly inhuman laugh. He panicked even more and began to run. As he did, something from behind him yelled, "Come back here!" in that same demonic and evil, threatening voice. He knew he couldn't trip and fall because if he did, that would be the end of him, and he somehow was aware, even through all of the panic and fear, he would lose his immortal soul. Whatever it was, was right on his heels the whole way, but he somehow made it back to his grandparents' house.

Of course, the door was locked. He began banging on it and screaming to be let in. His grandfather opened the door for him, holding a shotgun, and grabbed him and pulled him back inside the house with such force, Gianni was flung to the floor. His grandmother was trying to comfort him as his grandfather barricaded the door and locked all of the windows. His grandfather kept screaming about how he had brought evil to the house, and all of them were surely doomed. His grandmother explained, "This is exactly what we have been trying to warn you about. You shouldn't have gone out into this village at night." His grandmother insisted he go back to his bed, and so he did.

He was terrified to sleep and kept looking out the window while his grandfather yelled and cussed in some version of Italian Gianni had never heard before. His grandmother sprayed holy water everywhere from a giant spray bottle. Gianni was sent home within a day of the ordeal, and he was more than happy to go. When his grandparents said their goodbyes this time, it was with sadness, and he remembered feeling as though it was like they thought they'd never see him again or something.

Within weeks they had both died, both of them bizarre and gruesome deaths. His grandfather was shot at the village grocery store where he worked by a thief who stole nothing but his life. His grandmother was murdered in the bathtub of the home by some unknown and never caught assailant.

96

A TRUCKER'S TALE

A long-haul trucker named Jimmy sent this one to me. He was hauling a load from New Jersey out to California and said this encounter took place somewhere in Tennessee. He had pulled into a rest area, where he was able to park and sleep for the night or however long he needed to and use the facilities. He grabbed some dinner and took a shower and then headed off to his truck, excited to finally be able to get some rest. He made sure his doors were locked and windows rolled up, and he crawled into his little bed and went right to sleep.

Sometime in the middle of the night, he woke up to what sounded like some kind of animal outside his truck. It wasn't just outside his rig but close enough he could hear it. It sounded like a huge, snarling and barking dog. He jumped up and looked out the windows, truly thinking he was going to see a large and possibly rabid dog somewhere in the parking lot. He kept hearing it, but once he would look out the window where the sound was coming from, it would immediately change and sound like it was coming from the other side. This continued for a good twenty minutes. Finally he saw what looked to be a man walking through the parking lot, but something about this guy was off. The rest area was closed for the night, and only the lone gas station attendant was left. The attendant looked to be sleeping inside his little box there and none the wiser as to what was happening around him. Jimmy said he still heard the growling but not as loud and decided he didn't care enough to continue looking and figured this guy was a local who knew what he was doing.

He turned and fixed his bed back up and was about to open the door to "take a leak" right there outside this truck, but as soon as he turned around, much to his surprise, the odd-looking man was face-to-face with him through his window. The man was jiggling Jimmy's rig's door handles, but they were locked. He was snarling and foaming at the mouth, and his pants and shirt were tattered and stained with a bunch of blood. The white shirt and jeans almost looked like they were originally red, that was how much blood covered them.

Jimmy held back the urge to scream and said a few choice words and made a few threats to the guy about leaving his rig alone and going along his way before he got hurt. The man snarled again and half smirked and walked off. Jimmy was now concerned for the attendant and looked out the side window to make sure he didn't have to pull his gun to protect the poor guy, who was still sleeping and still had no clue what was going on. As he looked though, he was amazed and terrified all at once about what he was seeing. The man was completely and totally gone from sight. It had only been a split second since he had grabbed his gun and looked back out the window.

Getting angry now thinking someone in this town was playing a joke on a tired trucker, he grabbed his rifle and jumped out of his rig. Barking animals and strange drooling men be damned. He walked over to the attendant, all the while looking around, but saw no sign of the man or any type of animal at all let alone anything that could have been making those terrible and incessant noises. The attendant shot straight up when Jimmy knocked on his little booth, and when he saw the gun, he thought he was being robbed. Jimmy tried to explain himself but sounded just as much like the fool he was starting to feel like, and he was asked to leave the premises. He went a little further down the road and eventually slept.

What was it he had seen? Was the man the one making all of those strange animal sounds, or was the man the animal? Was it a shapeshifter? Was it one of the many murder victims along that highway come back for revenge? Jimmy didn't know and refused to speculate, and aside from recounting the story to me for this book, he said he never speaks of it. It's just too creepy and strange and brings up too many bad memories. His life went off the rails a bit after that night, and though it's back on track now, he never sets foot in that town in Tennessee again and certainly doesn't visit that rest area.

97

POSSESSED OR SIMPLY EVIL?

Callum was from London and lived a fairly normal life. He had a good marriage and five kids. All in all, his family was described as loving and happy. He was some sort of executive in the music industry, so he and his family were also quite wealthy. His wife and the children would visit her family in the United States for the summer, and he would come in August when he could get away from work. Callum and his wife, Moira, were also an extremely religious family and attended church services regularly.

After a decade of marriage though, Moira noticed a change in her husband when he came to visit her family one August in the States with her. She later said he was "Different. Like he had been hanging out with the devil or something." Up until that time things were always very normal and usual, and she never could figure out what had gone wrong that one summer in 1983. She would later find out that her husband wasn't as religious as he seemed or pretended to be, for whenever she would leave in June, he would immediately stop attending church until she returned in September. Of course, he visited with her when on vacation too.

Here is what happened after their visit to America in the summer of 1983. The whole month of August he just seemed "off." That was according to everyone who knew him well. He would go on late night walks and refuse to go to church. He would always claim some extremely important work thing came up on Sundays when it was time, and while it wasn't a big deal the first time or two, by the end of the summer, this coupled with everything else had his wife and the rest of his family extremely concerned. Callum would go for walks around his in-laws' home or for long drives in the middle of the night. He would come home at all hours of the morning and night. He had no explanation other than that he couldn't sleep and needed the fresh air. He also blamed it on missing London and said New York smelled funny. Speaking of smelling funny, even after he showered, Callum kind of always smelled like sulfur and oftentimes straight-up garbage too, throughout that whole August.

Once they got back to London, his wife demanded to know what was going on, but Callum would always laugh and tell her she was being paranoid. He continued blowing off church, though, and all at once was a violent and ornery man. His ego was seemingly out of control, and he became violent against his wife and kids. "He almost became like an animal," his wife remembered.

Eventually the church and its congregants became convinced Callum was possessed by the devil and decided he needed an exorcism. They gathered at his house, and upon his getting home from work one night, they strapped him to a chair and began to perform the rights of exorcism, as best they knew them. This caused Callum to start foaming at the mouth and growling. He was cursing and speaking in a language none of them had ever heard and certainly couldn't understand. He was telling secrets of the congregants though, and while they all tried to pretend they weren't hearing what he was saying, they all did. One by one they gave up and left until it was just Moira and her possessed husband strapped to a chair with several demons admittedly inside him. She tried to keep up with the prayers but was afraid for her life and the lives of her children.

She was right to be angry. You see, I have a friend who is a physical medium, and she conducted this interview with Moira after her husband, Callum, had murdered her and their kids that fateful night, the night of the exorcism when she was left in the house by her fellow supposedly Christian congregants with a man they knew had demons inside him. Callum ended up going to a sanitarium for the rest of his life, as he was deemed "insane" due to his actions leading up to that night and certainly afterwards.

While being held before trial, he would bite chunks out of other prisoners and eat the pieces among other unmentionable things. When asked when it all started, Moira says that now that she is on the other side and knows the whole story, she thinks it started that summer when he was murdering random women of the night while off on his excursions, his "drives and walks due to insomnia" while at her parents' house. Of course, she couldn't say for sure. She and her children have crossed into the light, and Callum, well, he is still alive and in the hospital for criminally insane people, the last one left in England. Of course, I was told this story in 1994, so I don't know if he is still there. Was Callum demon possessed or a man who was the victim of his own sin and lust? I can't tell you all what to believe, but I can say that I always believe what Spirit tells me in our conversations. I'm going to believe Moira.

98

IT FOLLOWED HIM HOME

One night Chris and a few of his high school buddies all decided to go to a local spot that had an urban legend attached to it. The legend was about a bunch of kids who were killed in a terrible school bus accident decades before and how some of those kids still haunt the bridge on the isolated road. The legend goes further to say that though the kids are innocent still, despite being lost souls now and still roaming the earth as spirits who are possibly very confused, if you drive a car like the one the drunk driver who caused their crash did, they will attack you in some way.

It was a very known legend throughout the town, and because Chris and all of his friends loved anything having to do with horror stories and ghosts, it made sense one of them would get that exact car that year. He had been saving up for it since before he got his license. The boys couldn't wait to ride down the road at midnight. It was said that as soon as you went under the underpass, that was when you would be attacked by this bunch of very young schoolchildren who would think you were their killer and attack your car.

Chris and his friends piled in, and they headed down the

allegedly haunted road and passed under the underpass right as the clock struck twelve. Nothing happened, at least not right then and there. They stayed around and waited and were so aggravated that the legend appeared not to be true that they even got out of the car and tried to lure the children to it by loudly proclaiming that they were, in fact, the men who had killed them and pointed to the car in order to prove it. Still, as the minutes ticked by, nothing happened.

They all went back to Chris's house, and because it was by now around two in the morning, his friends all spent the night. They went right to bed, but all of them had very restless sleep. They all dreamt of little kids following them down the road and attacking them with gleeful and even devilish smiles on their tiny little faces. The next day they all realized they had been dreaming almost the same exact dreams. The kids all looked different in their dreams though except one little boy. He had black hair and bright blue eyes, and in each of their dreams this little boy kept turning from a little boy and into a giant, terrifying demonic entity and back again.

Chris's mother woke up late and looked like she, too, hadn't slept. When the boys asked her about it, she told them she could feel some sort of presence in her room the night before, and several times she had woken up and saw, in the corner of her room, a little boy with bright blue eyes and black hair. She said it was eerie but not really scary because it was a little boy. She was a full believer of all things paranormal, so she decided to invite the little boy to stay in their house if he was lost but that he just couldn't lurk in the corner of her room anymore. Upon saying this, the boy grinned and disappeared. They tried moving, but the demonic activity continued, and their lives have never been the same since.

99

MISS MYRTLE

Miss Myrtle was a woman in our neighborhood when I was younger. Though an extremely pleasant old woman, she lived in the "haunted house" (which wasn't really haunted but was just run-down). She was also a shut-in, so when I would do my paper route, I knew to just go inside and bring the paper to her. She would give me a nickel for my troubles, but as someone who was always close to my grandmother, I would do it anyway and smile as I did.

One morning I went into Miss Myrtle's house to bring her paper, but she didn't greet me at the door like she usually did with my nickel and the offer of an umbrella in case it rained. I walked through her house and found her asleep in bed. I didn't want to wake her, as she looked so peaceful, and moved on about my day. The next day the same exact thing happened, and I was starting to get worried by now. I decided that if she was also sleeping the next day, that I would tell someone. The third day I went inside and found her asleep once again with the last two days' papers still unopened where I had left them. I was sad because now I knew something was wrong.

As I turned to walk out of her bedroom, I heard her say,

"Why so sad, child? Do you need an umbrella? It's supposed to rain later." I turned around in amazement. She wasn't dead after all, and she even gave me a quarter after muttering something about it having been a long couple of days. I said goodbye and left and went about my day.

As I was coming home from school later on though, when I passed Miss Myrtle's house, I saw the police there and a whole bunch of cars. I never understood what happened except I was told not to deliver her paper anymore, and I never saw her again.

As an adult, I asked my mother, and she told me that Miss Myrtle had been killed. She had been bludgeoned to death by her grandson when she wouldn't give him money and turned him away. My mom said she was concerned because I had been in the house after it happened three times to deliver her paper to her, but since I had never said anything, she assumed I hadn't seen anything traumatizing. I can't figure out why I didn't see any of the blood and gore on Miss Myrtle those three days I was there. I know her spirit was trying not to scare me on the third day, but why I didn't see anything at all on the other two, I'll never know.

IOO

THE CLAW

ary Christine works as a nurse, and when I told her
I was writing this book, she gave me this story and
insisted I put it in.

She said she was working a very slow shift one night in the
emergency department when she went to go and get some
coffee out of the vending machine. This one vending machine
was located next to a maintenance closet where many of the
nurses would go inside to sneak a cigarette with their fresh
vending machine coffee. As she waited for the coffee to pour
though, she saw out of the corner of her eye the maintenance
door opening, this in and of itself would have been no big deal,
but when she actually looked to see who was coming out of it,
there was nothing but a claw. A devilish and very large gnarled
and clawed hand was slowly opening the door of the maintenance room. Halloween had just passed, and she was sure that
someone was trying to play a prank on her, so she laughed to
herself and ripped the door open as fast as she could to catch
them in the act. Only, there was no one there. She screamed and
ran back to her station and never used that vending machine

again. She also stopped sneaking cigarette breaks in gloomy and scary closets throughout the hospital.

101

URBAN LEGENDS

At a sleepover one night, Carla and two of her best friends decided to play Bloody Mary. They turned off the lights in the bathroom, and they all went in. Carla's bathroom had one long mirror going along the one wall, and below it was the sink. All three girls were able to stand in front of the mirror and see themselves in the candlelight. Her one friend Ashley decided to audio record the entire thing on her cell phone so the girls could prove to people they did it and also so they could laugh at each other about how scared they were later.

The girls began the ritual and called for Bloody Mary and were giggling and laughing. They knocked on the mirror all at the same time and then each of them in turn. It was all fun and games until the candles were blown out by what seemed like a strong gust of wind. The bathroom door was closed, and it was in the middle of the house and therefore didn't even have a window in it that could have been left open. The girls started to scream, and all of them ran for the door all at once. They were locked in. This also should have been impossible because there was no lock on Carla's bathroom door. They screamed and cried and were in a complete and total panic.

Carla's mother finally raced into the room to open the bathroom door but not before Ashley dropped her cell phone, and the flash went off as though a picture were accidentally taken. The door opened, and Carla's mother was irritated and angry with the girls for lighting candles in the house and also for working themselves up so badly. She yelled for them to cut it out and go to sleep, and left the room.

The girls all lay in their sleeping bags, but it wasn't long before they all realized they had scratches on their arms and hands. They chalked this up to all of them having long nails and their desperate attempts at opening the bathroom door all at once. They didn't sleep much and had nightmares but eventually moved on from it, though they knew they'd never play Bloody Mary again.

About a week later Ashley was going through her photos on her phone when she turned completely pale and stopped in her tracks. She ran to Carla and their other friend who was there that night and showed them, and all three girls were terrified. They saw what looked like some sort of demonic woman attacking them with a very creepy and jagged, bloody-toothed smile on her face as she did it. The photo couldn't have been an accidental shot as the phone hit the floor either, as it was taken, seemingly, from the mirror itself. The angle showed the sides of the girls' faces as they struggled to make it out of the bathroom and this woman-thing attacking them while they did. They deleted the picture and never spoke of it again, but Carla admits she still has some strange things happening in her house and always feels an evil and sinister presence when in her bathroom.

Acknowledgments

I would like to first and foremost thank God and my Lord and Savior Jesus Christ for without his sacrifice I wouldn't be here today blessed to have my dreams of being a published author coming true.

Thank you to my husband, Ray for helping me along the way, picking me up when I get down on myself and loving me no matter what.

Kyle, Logan, Damien, Eliana and RJ, never stop believing in yourself or reaching for the stars. Jeff Borrin, thank you for always being honest with me and I know you're looking down on me, smiling and proud of who I've become. I'll miss you always until I see you again.

My mom, Carol, for believing in me and letting me use all of your encounters and horror stories for inspiration and content for this book.

All of my subscribers who have helped me achieve my goals one by one and little by little each day. Thank you all for being so supportive and kind, I wish I could thank you all by name.

About the Author

Gemma Jade was born and raised in Passaic County, New Jersey and has always felt drawn to the paranormal and supernatural world. She saw her first full bodied apparition at the age of four and was more interested in than terrified of it. Once she was old enough she started to seek answers. Gemma is of Native American and Irish descent and was fascinated by the old legends from both countries. She first  encountered the fairies and their magic when she was 7 and her paternal grandmother from the Irish old country would tell her of the myths and legends of "the Little Ones." Gemma was and continues to be lured by the unknown. She is also a clairvoyant and clairsentient psychic and credits this to her native American blood. She currently resides in Morris County, New Jersey.

Gemma has taken her research and search for all things paranormal, supernatural and unexplained to her youtube channel titled simply Gemma Jade. She has joined with Steve Stockton to livestream and communicate with other like minded individuals who are searching for the truth. They talk a lot about the missing in the woods, and of course the fae. Gemma's focus on her channel is also to bring light to missing person's cases happening all over the world both inside and out of the woods. She has even given a platform to her viewers where they cannot only feel safe in telling their own encounters, but also where they can communicate with like minded individuals in her community.

Join Gemma on her channel here: https://www.youtube.com/c/GemmaJadeYT

Also by Gemma Jade

Missing: The Fae Theory

Shadow Entities: Sleep Paralysis and Beyond